CONTRACTED

MARNI MANN

Visit my website at: www.MarniSMann.com
Cover Designer: Letitia Hasser, R.B.A Designs
Editor: Jovana Shirley, Unforeseen Editing, www.unforeseenediting.com
Proofreader: Judy Zweifel, Judy's Proofreading, and Kaitie Reister

ISBN-13: 978-1987406030

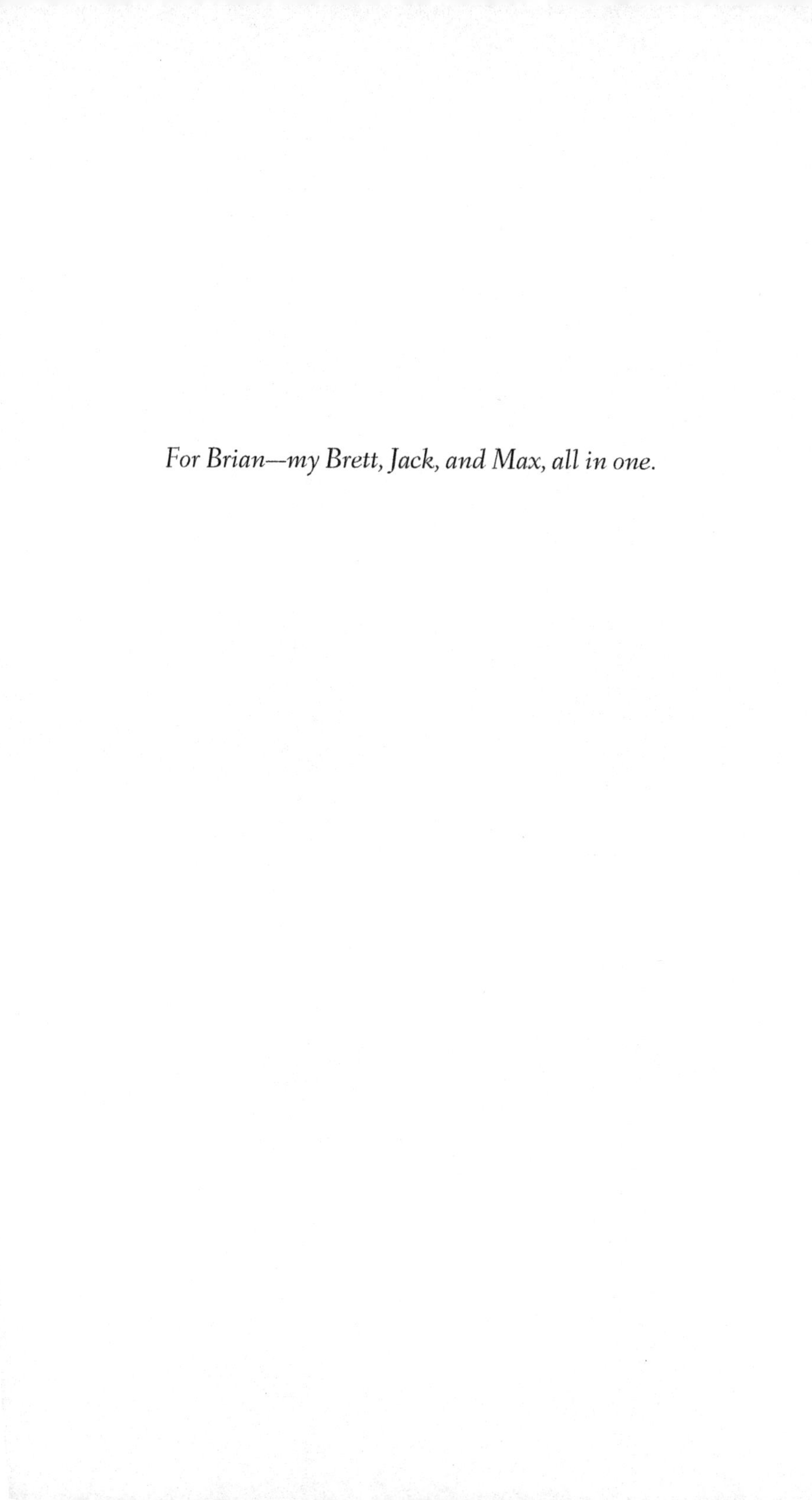

For Brian—my Brett, Jack, and Max, all in one.

PROLOGUE

MAX - TWO YEARS AGO

"GET UP," Brett said as he walked into his condo. He'd left me on the couch, watching the Heat game, to go to the lobby of his building and pick up the pizza he'd ordered. "We're going to James's."

As he went into the kitchen and grabbed a twelve-pack from the fridge, carrying it into the living room, I flipped off the TV. The look on my face told him exactly how I felt about the bullshit he'd just said to me.

"What?" he asked.

"Why the fuck are we going to James's?"

"I just saw her downstairs with her stylist, and they need my approval on some outfits."

James Ryne, Brett's newest client, had recently relocated to Miami and was renting a place in his building. America's sweetheart had escaped LA when a sex tape came out that ruined her whole career, taking her from one of the highest-paid actresses in Hollywood to unemployable. She'd hired our company, The Agency, to represent her, and Brett was now her agent.

Just because she worked with us didn't mean I wanted to

spend my downtime with her. I hardly got any time off. My musicians were as high-maintenance as Brett's actors. So, when I wasn't working, I wanted to relax and chill with my buddies.

Looking at some dresses wasn't that.

What it sounded like was fucking hell.

"And what am I?" I asked him, unsure of why he couldn't go to her place by himself. "A chaperone?"

"You're the fourth wheel."

I shook my head. "Not interested."

"Her stylist is hot as fuck. Trust me, brother."

Brett and I had the same taste in women. If he said she was hot as fuck, then I knew she must really be something to look at.

My feet slid off the cushion and dropped to the floor. "Now, I'm interested." I stood, taking the pizza boxes out of his hand, so he could carry the beer, and I followed him to the elevator. "It surprises me that you let the realtor move James into your building."

Jack and Scarlett, our other two business partners and best friends, also lived in downtown Miami high-rises. But not me. I didn't want to share walls or risk the chance of running into a client or an ex in the lobby. My fucking luck, I'd end up living above someone I'd dated, and I'd have to see her every goddamn morning at the gym.

That shit wasn't for me.

So, I'd bought a house on the water that was only a few minutes away. I didn't have a hell of a lot of land, but I had a direct view of Biscayne Bay, which was prettier than any of those fuckers had.

"Why?" he asked.

"You won't even bring the women you fuck back to your place because you don't want them to know where you live, but you'll let James be a neighbor."

"It's different."

I laughed as we stepped into the elevator, Brett hitting the button for James's floor.

"What's so funny?"

He'd forgotten we'd practically been brothers since we were kids. All these years later, and I could still see right through him.

"Something tells me you didn't mind running into her."

"Jesus, don't start with me."

I continued laughing and shook my head. "I'm not starting shit. I'm just saying, if a girl who looked like James lived by me, I wouldn't exactly be pissed off about it. But you're not me, and going down to her apartment isn't you."

"She's my client."

"So, that makes this different? If anything, it should make it worse."

"It makes her off-limits," he snapped. "We're going to her place to see some dresses. That's it."

He was getting worked up, proving my point even further, and that only made me laugh harder.

"Something you could do in the office," I said.

"You're fucking starting again."

"And, now, I'm dropping it."

Brett moved, so I couldn't see his face. He'd done that on purpose, which was the final bit of proof I needed.

Damn it, I loved it when I was right.

Eventually, he'd admit it since he sucked at keeping secrets from me.

We stepped out of the elevator and walked down the hall. When we reached the apartment, Brett knocked on the door, but James wasn't the one who answered it.

Jesus fucking Christ.

The chick standing in front of us was the hottest woman I'd ever seen. And that wasn't something I said often, considering I worked in the music industry and was surrounded by the most beautiful women in the world.

Brett said hello to her, and then he immediately walked into the apartment.

I didn't.

I stayed right where I was, not wanting to move a goddamn inch unless it was to get closer to her. I lifted my hand off the bottom of the pizza boxes and held it out. "Max Graham," I said.

As she shook it, I felt the lightness of her grip, the softness of her skin, the heat that poured through her fingers.

"Eve Kennedy, James's stylist."

She was too gorgeous to be a stylist. She should act or model or stand naked in my office, so I could look at her every moment of the fucking day.

"Brett and I are partners," I told her in case she thought I was the pizza delivery boy.

"Do you represent actors like Brett?"

"Nah, I work with musicians."

Her brows rose, and I could tell she was intrigued. "Really? I need to hear more about this. I'm a music junkie."

"How about you invite me in first?"

"Oh my God, I'm so sorry. I didn't mean to keep you standing in the hallway with food. Come in, please."

Once I got inside, I set the pizzas on the table, and I grabbed a beer that Brett had put in the fridge.

"James will be right out," Eve said to him. "She wanted to take a quick shower before she tried anything on."

I held the pizza box open for Eve. After she took a slice, I got one for myself, and then the three of us went into the living room. Brett and I sat on the couch, and Eve took a spot on the ottoman.

"I spoke to your team and kept their recommendations in mind when choosing each dress," Eve said to Brett, now in full business mode. "Several are black, but more than half are in jewel tones, which look incredible with James's skin tone..."

I stopped listening.

I wasn't interested in their conversation.

Instead, my mind was picturing Eve in the shower with water dripping down her skin. Her long, lean legs spread just enough that I could see underneath her pussy, her C-sized tits having the hardest fucking nipples.

When I realized she had caught me staring at her, I wedged the beer between my knees and took a bite of my slice. "When does the fashion show start?"

"Right now," James said.

I looked in James's direction but only for a few seconds because my gaze was being dragged back to Eve. She was speaking to Brett about the dress James had on, and I was watching the way her lips moved. How her tongue casually licked the inside corner of her mouth. How her eyes had turned so serious.

I wondered what her expression would be if I told her where I wanted to put my tongue.

"So, what do you think?" Eve asked Brett.

"It's good," Brett said. "Let's see the next one."

Neither of the ladies knew Brett like I did, so they had no idea he was doing everything in his power not to toss James over his shoulder and carry her to the closest bed. But his face and his voice told me how hard he was fighting that urge.

I wasn't too far behind him.

This fashion show needed to end. I was more interested in spending time with Eve than watching James put on these fucking dresses.

"How many will she be trying on?" I asked.

"Twelve," Eve said.

That meant we had eleven more to go.

The only good thing about this situation was that Eve's attention would be on James, and that meant my attention could be on her.

And that was what I planned to do the whole time my ass was on this couch—memorize every inch of her, every twitch of her lips, every freckle I was able to see.

Finishing off my slice of pizza, I grabbed my beer, kicked my legs onto the ottoman, not far from where Eve was sitting, and said, "Looks like we're going to be here for a while, so I might as well get comfortable."

"Tell me some music dirt," Eve said, smiling at me, as the two of us stood on the balcony outside James's apartment. "I've only ever worked with actors. I'm so out of the know when it comes to your industry."

Once James had finished trying on all the outfits, I'd gone out to get some air, trying to calm my fucking cock. It had been hard since dress two. The smirk Eve had given me during dress eight had me gripping the goddamn armrest of the couch, so she wouldn't find herself tossed over my fucking shoulder and stripped naked on the way to a bedroom.

She shifted positions, looking at me from the corners of her eyes, and it sent me her smell. It reminded me of a New England summer night that had hints of orange and leaves.

Those were some of my favorite scents.

Fuck.

I glanced away for a second, and then I turned toward her again, catching the tail end of her grin. "What do you want to know?"

"Who doesn't write their own lyrics? Who lip-syncs? You know...the dirt."

Even her voice was sexy.

It was a little raspy, like she'd been screaming from all the things my tongue was doing to her cunt.

"You're asking the wrong person," I said.

"No, I think I'm asking the right one. Something tells me you just need a little incentive to spill."

I heard the door slide open, and Brett stuck his head through the opening. "I'm going to head up."

"I'll be there in a little while," I told him.

Once the glass was closed, my eyes went back to Eve's lips and the long piece of dark hair hanging down next to it. The strands were caught in her gloss, and it took everything I had not to move them.

"What kind of incentive?"

The smile was back.

It was even larger now.

In the time I'd spent in this apartment, Eve had shown me she wasn't shy or timid at all. She was smart. Witty. And she had one hell of a mouth on her.

Before she could respond to my question, she needed to know something about me.

"I'm a forward kind of guy. I say what I want, and I rarely use a filter. In other words, I don't fuck around. So, just be straight-up with me."

"I don't fuck around either."

Finally, it sounded like I'd met my match.

"Tell me what's on your mind," she continued.

I would do that, but I was going to show her, too.

I gripped her waist, pulling her against my body so that she could feel how hard my cock was. Then, I leaned into her ear, knowing my words were going to vibrate across her skin. "Your lips. That's what's on my mind right now."

Her body tightened, telling me she wanted the same thing as me.

Her neck tilted back, and it gave me more of her skin to breathe against.

Then, she sighed into the hot Miami air. "If I give you my lips, are you going to stop there, or are you going to want more?"

My hands slid down her sides, keeping her body close to mine, and I tilted my hips forward, pushing my entire cock against her.

"Once I get a taste"—I inhaled, taking in her scent, as I brushed my nose across her hair—"I don't think I'll be able to stop."

ONE
EVE

"I FEEL like this dress is going to split open the second the cameras start flashing, and the entire world is going to see my bits," James, my longest client and best friend, said as I knelt below her, fixing the hem of her gown. "They've already seen me naked once. I won't survive another scandal like that again."

Our last fitting had been five days ago when she returned from Norway. She was four pounds lighter then, but she had needed to put on those pounds after an insane filming schedule where she had shot for eighteen hours a day. But it was weight I hadn't thought she'd put on so quickly; therefore, I hadn't factored it into my measurements.

Balmain gowns were known to be temperamental.

Still, I wasn't worried. I fought with dresses every day of my career, and this gorgeous piece of fabric wasn't going to win.

I reached inside my bag, grabbed my roll of Lycra, and got on my knees in front of her. "Listen, sister, I would never let that happen, but in order for me to fix this, you're going to have to spread your legs and let me in."

She widened her stance. "Do whatever you have to do."

Once I had my arms up and inside the dress, I looked under the skirt to see what I was doing and immediately pulled my face out. "Jesus, can you give me a little warning next time?"

"I figured you knew it was so tight, it wouldn't even hold a pair of panties."

I unraveled the edge of the Lycra and held it against her thigh, trying to slide my fingers up her hips. "It's a good thing you waxed because I don't even think a hair would fit in here." When I wasn't able to go any higher on her leg, I stood and moved in behind her to unzip the dress, helping her out of it, so I could wrap her properly.

"It's been almost four weeks since I've had sex," she whined. "FOUR. I'm so horny. If you keep touching me, I'm going to start moaning."

"I'm incredibly close to your vagina at the moment, so please don't; that'd just make things weird."

"Humping you would make things weird."

"Yeah, please don't do any of that either."

"Then, girl, you'd better hurry."

"I've never seen you this horned up before." I weaved the Lycra across the bottom of her navel and worked my way up to her ribs. "Do vibrators not work in Norway for some reason?"

"Brett's tongue has ruined my future with vibrators. They just can't compete."

I rolled my eyes, making sure she saw. "Poor girl."

James was engaged to her agent, Brett Young, and they were in the process of setting a wedding date. I had been with her at the bar the night she met him. And, since that first introduction, where she'd gone back to his place and had the best sex of her life, I'd been hearing about him nonstop.

She'd fallen for him so hard.

And I'd never seen her so happy.

After her ex-boyfriend had cheated on her, a sex tape of

James with a one-night stand had been released to the public, so happy was all I wanted for her.

"With four weeks of no action, your vagina must be practically closed up," I teased.

She gently slapped my arm as I smiled at her. Then, I wrapped three coats of Lycra around her torso. When I reached the dip of her thighs, I sliced the end and tucked it under the layers before I helped her get back into the dress. It zipped much easier now, and I could tell by her expression that she was much more comfortable with the fit.

"Tell me again why your fiancé-slash-agent wasn't allowed to visit you on set?"

"The director thought outside visitors would distract us."

I leaned down to straighten the hem. "Doesn't sex help you stay focused?"

"Please don't get me started. If you open that can of worms, I literally won't stop bitching. And, to make matters even worse, I've been back in the States for five days, and Brett's been so tied up with other clients that he wasn't able to fly here until tonight."

"Let's take the attention off your vag for just a second and point out that, based on your performance in Norway, you're going to catch the Academy's attention. So, my friend, four weeks of no sex and sucky vibrations are going to be all worth it."

"You might have a point."

"Now, you just have to get through the red carpet and the two-hour premiere, and then you can bang Brett in the limo on the way to the after-party."

"God, I love how you think."

I took a few steps back to look at the outfit as a whole. "Give me a minute. I need to focus."

Tonight's event was for a film James had shot over a year ago. The movie was edgy and angsty, and the plunging V-neck along with the gold-toned chains and eyelets throughout the bodice spoke to that so well. I'd requested the hairstylist to do a messy topknot, and the makeup artist had been told to do dark colors with lots of shadow.

But something was off.

"You're not happy," she said. She knew me so well. "Is it the four pounds I gained? Do I look—"

"It's the shoes."

I walked to the other side of her bedroom where I'd placed several rows of accessories on the floor. Even though James's outfit had been planned for weeks, I had to prepare for situations like this one, so I always took multiple options with me whenever I helped my clients get dressed.

I slowly scanned the alternatives, looking for ones that wouldn't compete with the dress but wouldn't be understated either. On the second row, all the way at the end, I came across a pair of Prada—gold leather peep-toes with a T-strap and a front platform. They were exactly what I was looking for.

"Come here, goddesses," I said to the heels as I lifted them into my hands. "Valentino is coming off," I told James, returning to her side. "And these little beauties are going on."

She held on to the wall while I did the quick exchange, and then I stepped back once more to see the new look.

"Damn, I'm good."

She put her hands on her waist and turned to show me her profile, twisting a little more to reveal the back before she faced me again. "Yeah?"

"Definitely."

"So, this is the final, *final*?"

Since there wasn't a mirror in here, I said, "Go take a look and you tell me."

I followed her into her large walk-in closet and stood behind her while she checked out her reflection in the full-length mirror.

She moved, observing herself in every angle, and then her eyes caught mine. "This might be one of your best creations."

"I don't know if it's my *best*, but I certainly nailed it."

She gave herself a final glance, and then she turned toward me. "As long as I don't sit, breathe, or put anything in my mouth that will cause the Lycra to expand, it'll be the perfect night."

"It's just the Hollywood premiere of one of your biggest movies ever. Why would you be expected to do any of those things?"

She laughed. "You're coming to the after-party, right?"

Once I left here, I had another client to dress for an entirely different event. Then, I had to stop by a client's house to prep her for a two-week press tour where she needed several outfits for each day she'd be gone. I'd be done just in time to meet James at the hotel where the after-party was taking place.

"I'll be there," I told her.

"Good." Her grin grew. "Now, you need to tell me all about your weekend in Nassau. You didn't say much about it when we were talking through text, so I need all the details."

I closed my eyes for the briefest of seconds, filled my lungs, and slowly released the air with a moan. "We fucked for three days straight—on the beach, in the hammock, in the back of the SUV on the way to dinner. At dinner. It was perfection."

"At dinner?"

"Ohhh, yes. Right on the table while we were in a private room."

"Did the suite not come with a bed?"

I chewed the corner of my lip as I thought about that night. "Beds are old school. We prefer walls and sand and leather seats and tables."

"Suddenly, I feel so vanilla."

"Don't," I told her. "What you and Brett have is amazing. There's no need to change a thing."

"And you and Max?"

I shrugged. "We're just us."

"But, at some point, aren't you going to get tired of being the mistress to his job?"

She'd never said anything like that before, and we talked about Max all the time. His work schedule wasn't something I ever complained about, so I wasn't sure where this was coming from.

"You know Max and I aren't anything like you and Brett. Work comes first. That's the arrangement we've had forever."

"But aren't you ever going to want more?"

By *more,* if she meant seeing Max later at the after-party, then I was getting that.

For now, that was all I needed.

"I'm certain, by the end of the night, when he's fucking the shit out of me, I'll be screaming *more* so loud that you and Brett will hear me all the way at your house in the Hollywood Hills."

She burst out laughing. "Sometimes, I just want to shake you."

I grabbed her fingers and squeezed them. "Stop worrying about me. I'm the best I've ever been. Work is exploding, I'm getting new clients every day, and I'm traveling the world. I can't ask for much more than that." I lifted her hand into the air and twirled her in a circle, taking one last gaze at this stunning look. "Now, it's time for you to go, or you'll be late to your own movie."

"Eve—"

"Come on, the limo is outside, waiting for you," I said, cutting her off and leading her through the bedroom where I grabbed her clutch off her bed and then brought her into the foyer. I released her hand to open the door for her. "I'll see you in a couple of hours. You look gorg." I ushered her down the first step. "Remember, don't breathe, and you'll be just fine."

She turned to blow me an air kiss. "Bitch."

I gave her ass a hard slap, and then I rushed back inside and shut the door, going straight to her bedroom to pack up everything I had brought.

Just as I was boxing up the last pair of heels, my cell rang. I checked the screen, seeing that it was Lorrie, the makeup artist who had worked on James tonight. She'd left here over an hour ago, but I'd texted her shortly after and told her to call when she had a second.

"Hey, girl," I said into the phone.

"What's up?"

"I know it's last minute, but I wanted to see if you had any plans tonight."

"For you, I'm always free."

I smiled as I moved to the jewelry and began to bag it up. "I won't be far from your place, so I can pick you up around eleven."

"I'll see you then," she said and hung up.

Lorrie was on board.

That meant tonight was definitely going to be a good time.

TWO
MAX

I RUSHED up the short staircase of our company's private jet and sat in the seat across from Brett, setting my briefcase on the table beside us.

He hung up with whomever he had been speaking to and said, "You're late."

I checked my watch. Twenty minutes was nothing. Hell, in the music industry, that was considered early.

"You're lucky I didn't hit any traffic," I told him. "Then, I really would have been late."

He shook his head. "Selfish motherfucker."

I flipped him off and opened my briefcase, taking out the folder that I'd grabbed from my desk this morning. It held the latest version of the Ray-Ban contract that Brett and I had been negotiating for weeks. Brett represented the husband, and the wife was one of my clients. Ray-Ban wanted the couple for an international ad campaign. Since our company, The Agency, was sectored into different departments—acting, music, and sports—and Brett and I didn't have the same commission structure, the contract had to be accepted by both sides. That was why coming to an agreement had been taking much longer than normal.

Still, it didn't matter how long it took. There was fifteen million dollars on the line. We had to get this shit right and make sure all parties were taken care of.

Brett nodded toward the folder. "You'd better have something good to show me. The last set of figures they sent were fucking bullshit."

"We're going to need some scotch before I let you read it."

"Christ." He stuck his hand into the air, calling over the flight attendant.

As she approached us, she said, "Can I get you something else for breakfast, Mr. Young?"

The table had been stocked with bottled water, freshly squeezed orange juice, and a platter of fruit and muffins.

"Scotch, just a finger's worth," Brett said.

"And for you, Mr. Graham?"

Her lips were red and glossy, her bright white teeth gnawing on the inside corner of the bottom one. They looked extra pouty and plumper than usual.

She was trying so fucking hard to keep my attention on them.

"Two fingers' worth." I pointed at Brett. "Pour him the same."

"I'll be more than happy to."

She stood at our table for a second longer, giving me the sexiest smile, before she moved to the back of the plane.

"She's hot."

My eyes connected to Brett's. "Not hot enough," I replied.

We both laughed, knowing how true that statement was.

"Where are you headed after LA?" he asked.

I pulled out my phone, clicking on the itinerary my assistant had put together. "Nashville, Las Vegas, Denver, Chicago, Dallas, and then home."

"Are they all tour stops?"

Eight of my clients were currently headlining world tours, and three more were about to start. It was going to be a busy fucking season.

"Three are," I told him. "Las Vegas is a photo shoot, and I'm meeting with a label in Nashville."

"Isn't that why you're flying to LA? To meet with a label?"

I took a piece of pineapple off the tray and popped it into my mouth. "Yeah, and I'm about to pulverize those fuckers."

His eyes narrowed. "For which client?"

"Talia, my ex-reality star, who won the singing competition." I tossed in a chunk of melon and chewed it. "The show wants a cut of all her future earnings. They've been milking her for five fucking years, and I'm putting a stop to that shit today."

"Isn't that all spelled out in her contract?"

After all the hours I'd put in, trying to get Talia out of this goddamn mess, it felt incredible to know this was a war I was going to fucking win.

"Her contract specifically states, they only get a cut of her future R and B royalties."

"So?"

"She wants to record a country album."

The flight attendant dropped off two tumblers of scotch and asked if we needed anything else.

I shook my head and waited for her to leave again before I added, "They can't fuck with a genre she's not under contract for."

He lifted his glass but didn't drink from it. "You're positive?"

Brett, Jack, and I had gone to law school, so we could read our clients' contracts and write our own. Therefore, I didn't need to consult our in-house counsel—an attorney The Agency employed because the agents who worked for us didn't have backgrounds in law. But, just to get a second opinion, I'd asked him, and he'd confirmed exactly what I thought.

"By a million percent," I told Brett.

"And you're going to tell the label today?"

I clinked my glass against his. "I can't wait to see their fucking faces." I took a drink of the scotch. "In two days, Talia and I are getting on this plane and going to Nashville where she's going to sign one of the largest contracts I've ever negotiated."

"That's my fucking boy."

I smiled like a man who was about to get his dick sucked.

By the end of the night, I would be.

"Now, let's talk about Ray-Ban," I said.

"I hope you have some good news for me."

I took the stack of papers out of the folder, flipped to the seventh page, and showed him the number that was circled at the bottom. "Is that figure a little closer to what you're looking for?"

It wasn't close.

It was six points higher than what he'd asked for.

"Fucking Christ." He laughed. "You're on fire."

I set the contract on the table and reclined in my seat just as the plane began to move toward the runway. "Nah," I said. "It's just what I do."

There were cameras flashing in the front of the building and paparazzi littering the entire goddamn entrance. I didn't want to deal with any of that shit, so I had my driver pull up to one of the side doors. Once we came to a stop, I climbed out of the back, straightening my jacket and tie before I slipped inside.

As I made my way down the hallway, I checked the time. It was a little after midnight.

I'd arrived here later than I wanted. That was because the meeting with the label had lasted longer than I intended.

When I'd pointed out the hole in Talia's contract, the label's legal team had threatened a lawsuit. They'd put up a hell of a fight, and that'd only made me go at them harder.

The arguing had gone on for hours.

Finally, Talia had walked out of that building as an unsigned artist, getting everything the both of us wanted for her. So, we had gone to dinner to celebrate and then for a drink at my favorite bar in LA. While we had been there, something unexpected had happened.

My ex had walked in.

Kristin Evans.

She wasn't just a girl I'd fucked a few times.

She was the girl I'd dated all through high school and college. Whom I'd been with up until the guys, Scarlett, and I moved to Miami to start The Agency. Whom I'd proposed to and thought I was going to spend the rest of my life with until she broke things off the night before we were supposed to go to Florida.

She was the girl who had scarred my fucking soul.

Tonight wasn't the first time I'd run into her since she ended our relationship. But it was the first time I'd seen her since she returned from Brazil where she'd spent the last three years.

Once I'd had my driver take Talia home, I had gone over to Kristin's table. It had taken me a long time to get to the point where I could do this, where I could talk to her about something other than the way she had broken things off. Over the years we'd discussed what had happened, and I began to understand her side.

I'd forgiven her.

Just because all of this time had passed didn't mean I'd stopped caring. Our history was too thick to even consider doing that. So, I'd sat in the stool across from hers, and we'd caught up. Three years without seeing each other meant we'd had a shitload of ground to cover.

When I had seen how late it was getting, I'd had my driver take me here.

Now, I was walking down another hallway, rounding the corner and heading toward the noise. There had to be at least a few hundred people gathered at the hotel to celebrate, so it wasn't hard to find the spot where they were all hanging out.

What was hard to find was the beautiful brunette I was meeting.

I circled three-quarters of the room, giving my congratulations to those who had been honored at tonight's event, and then I went to the only section I hadn't covered.

That was where I spotted her.

She sat on a barstool, facing away from me, her dark hair hanging down her back, hints of her tan skin peeking through the long locks. I wanted to wrap those strands around my fucking wrist and pull them until her neck was exposed. Once I had it open, I wanted to press my lips against the center of it and lick all the way to her mouth.

I needed a taste.

Even if it was just a small one.

I made my way toward her and stopped when my chest grazed the back of her arm. Then, I gripped the bottom cushion she was sitting on, my thumb rising just enough to brush across her ass.

She stiffened once she felt me.

As she went to look over her shoulder, I leaned my lips into her ear and said, "Fuck, I've missed this body."

The tension began to leave her, and a smile filled the corner of her mouth. "I was just thinking about your cock."

Eve liked to fuck as much as I did.

And, for the last two years, she'd gotten a lot of my dick.

My finger slowly moved up her side, her grin widening the higher I climbed, tiny goose bumps growing over her flesh.

"Baby, you look gorgeous tonight."

Her eyes dipped down my suit. "You don't look so bad yourself."

"Let's get out of here," I demanded.

She swiveled a little more, giving me her whole face, one that was so fucking exquisite, my cock stretched against my zipper, throbbing. "I have a surprise for you."

There were sexy lips all over Miami. A set on the plane that had been arousing enough to make me rock hard.

But none compared to the ones I was looking at now.

She ran her tongue across the middle of them, showing me how wet she could get them, how pointed she could make the tip.

I could almost feel it lapping across my crown, and I fucking hissed because of it.

"What's the surprise?" I asked.

"Me," a woman said from behind me.

I turned and saw a blonde sitting directly in back of me. She was wearing a low-cut dress that advertised her handful-sized tits, a face that was decently hot, and a hungry set of eyes that told me she wanted to fuck.

"I'm your surprise," the blonde added.

My gaze slipped down her body, gradually making its way back up.

"Now, it's time to get out of here," Eve said in my ear.

It had been two weeks since our trip to the Bahamas.

Since I'd touched her.

Since I'd been inside her cunt.

Since I'd kissed her cheek and whispered a good morning.

I'd missed it.

All of it.

And I was long overdue for the taste I was going to get.

But it looked like I was getting more than that tonight.

"Why are you so good to me?" I growled.

"I just love to surprise you, and I love the rewards you give me whenever I do it."

My arm slid around her waist, my palm traveling down the crack of her ass. "You're going to get several tonight."

Eve's fingers linked through mine, and she said, "Then, let's go."

As she led me out of the bar, I took a quick peek to make sure the blonde was trailing behind us.

And she was.

THREE
EVE

MAX'S DRIVER dropped the three of us off in my driveway, and I led them inside the small house I rented in West Hollywood.

The place was an utter disaster.

The living room was full of clothing racks. My couch was covered in shoeboxes. The top of my fireplace and kitchen table held jewelry and clutches. I really needed an office or a warehouse to hold everything I pulled from the showrooms. I just didn't have time to look for one.

"You guys want a drink?" I said over my shoulder, heading toward the kitchen.

Besides a jar of pickles, some coffee creamer, and condiments, I had nothing to give them to eat. But I was always well stocked with liquor, and I had a decent selection of beer and wine.

"I'll take whatever you have," Max said.

He was extremely picky about what he drank. Beer or scotch—that was all he liked. I knew his answer hadn't been specific because, right now, he didn't care about what I got for him to drink. The only thing Max wanted was Lorrie and me naked.

I opened the fridge, grabbing an IPA for him and the bottle of white I'd opened last night for me, and I poured the wine into a stemless glass.

"I'll have one of those," Lorrie said from the other side of the kitchen.

I looked over my shoulder to see which drink she was referring to and saw her point to the wine.

Turning back around, I reached for a second glass, and that was when Max moved in behind me. He clasped my waist with one hand, circling the bottle of beer with the other. After he took a sip, he pressed his lips against my neck. They were cold on the outside. But, as his mouth opened, his kiss deepening, his skin turned hot.

"Fuck, you taste good," he said.

I closed my eyes and took a breath, savoring how incredible he felt.

I'd missed him.

So much.

"I was planning on bringing you back here tonight," he said, "filling your bathtub, putting the both of us in it, and then taking turns rubbing each other's bodies. I'll save that for your next trip to Miami."

I leaned my head back, pushing it against him as my chest melted from his description. "Next time. Definitely."

With his mouth still on me, he touched the beer bottle to my bare back.

"*Ahhh,*" I groaned, the freezing glass causing a wave of chills to break out across my flesh.

He dragged it higher, stopping when he reached the top of my shoulders. I shivered as the condensation dripped down the center of my spine.

"Leave the wine on the counter," he ordered, his lips hovering above the outer edge of my ear. "You're not going to have time to drink it." When he exhaled, my nipples turned hard, rubbing into the thin fabric of my dress. "Neither is she."

My eyes opened, and I released the glass. My hands then slid to the edge of the counter, gripping it with all the strength I had.

He bunched my hair together, wrapped it around his fist, and pulled until my neck leaned all the way back. "It's been two weeks since I've seen you. Two weeks of fucking torture."

I filled my lungs, air swishing through my body, mixing with the tingles that had already been exploding in my stomach. And I was so turned on; wetness was pooling in my panties.

I took a step back, and it locked our bodies together, his cock pressing against my upper back.

I felt the length.

Width.

How hard it was as it ground into me.

"Fuck yes," I sighed.

"That's what you do to me. You make my dick so fucking hard, it's throbbing to be inside you." His mouth lowered, and he nipped at my skin.

I gasped, "Max."

"Goddamn it, I want you." He slipped his hand across my thigh and slowly made his way up until he was resting his palm against the middle of my navel. "Get over here," he said, and I knew he was speaking to Lorrie. "I'm so busy thinking about your cunt that I've ignored the present you got me." That was when I knew he was talking to me.

"You're going to like her," I told him. "She's extremely submissive."

"Mmm," he grunted.

I heard her come closer.

I smelled her flowery perfume.

It wasn't anything like Max's cologne. His scent was powerful. A combination of leather and spice.

It fit him perfectly.

He took Lorrie's hand and connected it with mine. Then, he turned my body, so I faced her. "I want you to take Eve to her bedroom. I want both of you to get naked. And then I want the two of you waiting for me on the bed." When Lorrie didn't immediately respond, he said, "Do it now."

FOUR
MAX

WHILE THE BLONDE led Eve through the living room, disappearing down the hall, I stayed in the kitchen. I held my beer and used my other hand to take out my phone and scroll across the screen. It had vibrated several times since we arrived at Eve's place, and I had to make sure none of the messages were an emergency.

They weren't, but knowing it would take them a few minutes to get undressed, I checked out the recent emails that had come in. One was from Scarlett, referencing a business meeting that she needed Brett, Jack, and me to attend. It was scheduled for a few weeks from now when all of us would be back in Miami.

I quickly left that screen and opened my text messages.

There were multiple.

Only one caught my attention.

The one from Kristin.

Kristin: Lunch tomorrow?

It hadn't even been two fucking hours since I left her at the bar, and she was already reaching out.

I shook my head, closing the message instead of replying to it, and I shoved my phone back into my pocket. I downed the rest of the beer, leaving it on the counter, and then I made my way toward Eve's bedroom.

As I stopped in the doorway, I saw both women lying in the middle of the bed. They'd kept their heels on, and they were wearing nothing besides their jewelry.

What a fucking sight.

The blonde was hot as hell. Confident. Sexy. Her eyes connected with mine, and she leaned into Eve's neck, kissing it like I had in the kitchen.

My cock got even harder.

Still, it didn't matter what the blonde looked like—not her body, not her face. Not even the goddamn sounds she was making. Because she had nothing on Eve.

That girl and her body were fucking perfect.

She had tits that were real, that fit in the palms of my hands. An ass with just the right amount of thickness, giving me something to grab. Legs that were long and toned, the right length to wrap all the way around me.

And that fucking face.

It was more gorgeous than any woman The Agency represented.

Any woman who appeared on the screen.

Any woman who was contracted in this business.

And it was mine.

Staying in the doorway, I loosened my tie and tossed it on the chair that wasn't far from where I stood. My jacket followed, and I continued to strip until everything was off.

While I walked to the bed, I stroked my cock.

The blonde eyed my dick. "You're a lucky girl," she said to Eve.

She was right about that.

But being able to put this cock inside Eve's cunt made me just as lucky.

Reaching the end of the mattress, I said, "Get over here."

They crawled to me, clasping their hands around my shaft, one higher than the other, and they pumped me several times before Eve's lips surrounded my crown. She sucked the tip, swiveling across the outer edge, dipping toward my balls and back up. Each time she reached the head, she would tease the slit with the tip of her tongue.

I fisted her hair, tightly holding it, and I used it to guide her. With each dip, she took in more of me.

The blonde's hands were now on my thighs, and she was sucking my balls. She could only fit in one, but she gave it plenty of suction, her tongue running across it as fast as Eve was bobbing.

As they waited for my next order, I felt their stare on me, and I heard their soft moans muffled from their mouths being so full.

Just a little more.

Only because they were so fucking good at what they were doing.

"Deeper," I growled, letting Eve take in as much as she could but knowing she was capable of more.

I was nearing the back of her throat.

But I wasn't quite there yet.

"My turn," the blonde said, eager to take over.

Eve's eyes connected to mine, and I said, "Let her have my cock and come sit on my face."

I could tell Eve liked that response.

They both did.

Eve's lips left my shaft, and I walked around to the side of the bed and climbed into the middle of it. Eve crawled up my body until her pussy was hovering over my mouth. The second I stuck out my tongue, getting ready to lick the length of her, I felt the blonde's lips surround the tip of my dick.

"Fuck," I hissed.

I had everything I wanted—a gorgeous cunt in my face and a hot, wet mouth sucking my cock.

"Take it all in," I told the blonde. I knew she wouldn't be able to—not even Eve could deep-throat the whole length—but I wanted more than what she was giving me.

While the blonde worked her way down, I pointed my tongue and focused on the top of Eve's clit, sticking two fingers into her pussy.

"Max," Eve groaned, fisting my hair to bring me in even closer.

She smelled so fucking good.

She tasted even better.

Her wetness dripped onto my tongue every time I surrounded her. She was bucking, riding out every flick I gave her, every grind of my fingers as I went in to my bottom knuckles. I twisted my hand just slightly before I pulled out to do it again.

And, while I ate the pussy I'd been thinking about for the last two weeks, the blonde was lowering to the center of my shaft and sliding back up, repeating the pattern as she cupped my balls.

"Mmm," I moaned into Eve's cunt.

Each syllable that left my mouth vibrated across her, and I could tell it made her even more sensitive.

I could also tell how close she was getting.

Her hips were moving faster. Her fingers were pulling my hair even harder.

Soft groans were draining from her lips.

"Let me feel it," I told her. "Right on my fucking tongue." I added in more pressure while my fingers drove in and out of her core. "Give it to me, Eve. Right now."

It only took a few more licks until the softness in her voice was gone, and I was sure the neighbors could tell she was coming.

It didn't cause the blonde to slow down at all. If anything, Eve's sounds only made her suck faster. And, with her lips on my crown, her hand was pumping the bottom.

It wasn't enough.

I needed more.

Now that I'd tasted the cum from Eve's orgasm, I wanted my dick soaking in it.

So, once she stilled, I lifted her pussy off my face, and I set her on the bed. "Get on your back," I told her. Holding the base of my cock, I pulled out of the blonde's mouth and moved in between Eve's legs, resting the backs of her knees across the top of my shoulders. From this angle, I had the perfect view of Eve's body, and I wanted to see what it would look like with the blonde on top of her, the two of them coming together, so I said, "Go put your cunt on Eve's mouth."

The blonde moved fast, kneeling to the side of Eve's head, her hands running down her tits while her pussy straddled Eve's tongue.

"Fuck yes," I roared. "Now, that's the fucking sight I want to see."

I pumped my cock several times with my hand as I stared at Eve's opening. Once she and I had made things exclusive, which had happened a few months into our relationship, and I was sure she was on birth control, I'd stopped wearing a condom. So, as I held her ass high off the mattress and positioned myself underneath her, I rubbed my unwrapped cock over the outside of her pussy. Her wetness immediately coated my tip. Her heat teased me. So did the tightness that I knew was waiting for me inside her cunt.

The blonde's eyes didn't leave mine as her hands slid to Eve's nipples. That was one of the most sensitive places on her body. And, when she was coming, she liked to have them squeezed.

"Bite them," I ordered.

A smile pulled at the blonde's lips while her hips rocked over Eve's face. "Yes, sir."

Submissive, just like Eve had said.

And I liked giving demands.

We were going to get along just fine.

As her teeth clamped down on Eve's nipple, I thrust inside her pussy, giving her my full length in one stroke.

"Max!" she yelled, her voice dripping in pleasure, muffled from being nose deep inside the blonde.

Her pussy quivered around me.

"*Fuuuck*," I growled.

She felt so fucking good.

I pulled out and punched in again.

"Yes!" Eve screamed, causing the blonde to buck. "God, I missed your cock."

I knew she was reacting from the combination of the blonde's teeth on her nipple, from my dick, and from having a beautiful pussy on her mouth. And I knew she loved what she was getting from us, so I didn't stop, and I sure as hell didn't slow down.

"Harder," I barked at the blonde, rearing my hips back and pushing my way through Eve's tightness. "Do you want to come?"

"Yes," she moaned.

"Then, ride her fucking face."

I continued to slide through Eve's heat as fast and as deep as I could, keeping her legs spread wide so that I could pound her as hard as I wanted.

And I did.

Relentlessly.

With each stroke, I tilted my hips forward to reach the spot that would bring her closer to that build.

"Oh my God," Eve groaned. "That feels fucking incredible."

Her fingers were stabbing the blanket, and her heels were slapping against my shoulders.

"Lick the ends of her nipples," I told the blonde. "And put your hand on her clit."

She did as I'd ordered, and I picked up my speed. When I was all the way in, I circled my hips several times, grinding my dick inside her, before I pulled out to the tip and repeated the motion.

As the blonde leaned across Eve's body, her fingers stroking that gorgeous cunt, I saw the top of the blonde's ass. Her cheeks were thick, just how I liked them. It would be hot as hell to have that ass facing me, spread nice and wide while my cock was buried inside it.

But, if I fucked the blonde, I'd have to put on a condom.

I wasn't about that right now. Not after being inside Eve without one.

Besides, I could feel how close she was getting. As she neared the edge, her pussy clamped down on me even harder. And, with the sounds coming out of the blonde, I knew she wasn't far behind.

Neither was I. Not with all that tightness and heat that was swallowing me.

"Faster," I said to the blonde as she circled the middle of Eve's clit. "Eve, make her fucking scream."

"Ah," the blonde groaned, her back arching, tits bouncing each time she rocked her hips. "That feels so good."

Eve's hand lifted from the blanket, and it moved behind the blonde's cunt. When I saw her arm slide back and forth, I knew she was finger-fucking her.

This view just kept getting better.

"Max," Eve said, her voice even more muffled now, "I'm so close."

I lifted her several inches higher, using this new space to lengthen my stroke, and I pummeled into her.

My balls began to tighten.

"Fuck," I groaned.

"Oh God," Eve moaned back. "That fucking cock of yours."

"*Yesss!*" the blonde shouted after several seconds.

Holding on to Eve's thighs, I reared back before I buried myself all the way. Using small, shallow thrusts, I pumped out the first stream.

"Max!" Eve shouted.

From the way the blonde was breathing, I knew the three of us were getting off at the same time.

"That's it," I told Eve. "Squeeze all of that cum out of me." The blonde's eyes connected to mine, and I said, "I want your pussy juice to coat her fucking face."

"*Ahhh,*" the blonde responded.

I followed her arm down Eve's navel to the top of her clit where wetness was soaking each of her fingers.

Jesus.

Eve was fucking dripping.

That was another sight I loved to see.

A second wave shot through me, followed by a load of cum that went straight into her cunt.

When I was finally empty and the two of them quieted, I slowed my movements to a stop. Both women stared at me from the bed. Their skin was flushed. Their hair a mess. Their hands all over each other. Eve's face was as wet as the blonde's fingers.

They were waiting for my next order.

A smile filled my lips as I carefully pulled my cock out of Eve. Staying on my knees, I dropped her legs off my shoulders and moved several inches to the side, so I was between both girls.

I nodded toward the blonde. "Come clean my cock."

She returned the smile as she crawled toward me, her tongue sticking out before it even landed on me. Then, she swiped it across my entire shaft. Each flick licked more of the wetness off, a mix of both Eve and me.

And, as she did, my eyes locked with Eve's.

There was something besides satisfaction that filled her face.

An expression I knew all too well.

"You missed me," I said. Her eyes gave me the answer I was after, so I said, "When she's done sucking you off my dick, I'm going to fuck you again."

I could tell those were the words she wanted to hear. Once they resonated, she dropped her hand between her legs and brushed her clit, as though she were wiping it off. "I have a request."

"I make no promises."

She grinned. "I want you in my ass."

Jesus Christ.

That dirty fucking mouth was all mine.

"Hey," I said to the girl who was bobbing over my cock. "While I fuck Eve's ass, you're going to put your cunt on my face, and I'm going to eat you until you come."

The girl looked up at me, eyes wide and a little watery as she tried to take more of me in. She pulled back to say, "Yes, sir."

I glanced at Eve.

She'd done good.

The blonde was the most perfect fucking present.

FIVE
EVE

MY EYES OPENED as I heard my phone ding, the sound I'd set specifically for text messages. Since my clients often needed me all hours of the day and night, I pushed myself out of bed in search of my cell. I hadn't taken it out of the clutch I wore to the after-party, so that was what I looked for in my room. I found it on the chair, hidden beneath Max's suit. Quickly opening the small bag, I gripped the plastic case and scrolled the screen with my thumb.

There were multiple messages. The most recent one was from James.

James: You're forgiven.
Me: Did I fuck up?
James: You left the after-party without saying good-bye. Bitch.
Me: I was on a mission to get laid.

I looked up and glanced toward the bed. Lorrie had left several hours ago, so Max was the only one in it. He was lying on his stomach, the comforter resting across the top of his ass.

Just enough sun came through the windows to highlight the muscles in his back, the dips where they began and ended, each edge so well defined.

God, that man was so fucking hot.

James: I figured since I noticed Max had disappeared, too. How was the reunion?

Me: Hot as fuck.

James: Then, tell me again why you wouldn't want to wake up next to him every morning? And why you two still spend so much time away from each other?

Me: Jesus, woman. It's not even nine yet, and I only went to bed a few hours ago. You can start the interrogation after I've downed some coffee and more dick.

James: Really? Because, if this were reversed, you'd want a fifteen-sentence answer, and you wouldn't settle for anything less.

Me: I never said I was fair. I'll text you later. Love you, bitch.

I brought the phone over to the bed and set it on the nightstand, climbing under the sheets and blanket. The movement caused Max's eyes to open, his stare showing me that he'd woken up hungry. By the way he reached for me, I knew it wasn't food he was after.

"What time do you have to head out?" I asked as he flipped me onto my side, pulling my back against his chest.

Several of his exhales hit my shoulder before he said, "What time is it?"

"Quarter to nine."

"I have about an hour." He kissed across the top of my back. "Are you seeing clients this morning?"

"No, but I have a ton of prepping and planning to do."

I'd cleared my entire schedule today in hopes that he would, too.

I should have known better.

Work came first.

That was the rule, and it had been since the moment we started dating.

Therefore, hoping he'd give me the whole day had only been setting myself up for disappointment.

Still, I couldn't help but think of the question James had asked me yesterday.

"But aren't you ever going to want more?"

Max's hand drifted down my side and around to my ass, squeezing the bottom of my cheek. "You were so fucking good to me last night."

I had known he'd like having Lorrie join us.

She wasn't the first woman I'd shared with him. I'd brought in many over the years.

Some were for me; others were for him.

Lorrie was for the both of us.

"I thought you deserved a little treat."

"Treat?" he repeated, clutching my ass even harder, kissing the back of my neck. "For making me wait two weeks to see you?"

I laughed as he bit the bottom of my ear. "I've been traveling nonstop since I got back from the Bahamas. I didn't have time to go to Miami; you know that."

"Doesn't mean I liked it."

I smiled. "Are you saying you missed me?"

"You know the answer to that. Just don't make me wait so long next time."

"Yes, sir," I said, mimicking Lorrie, who had said that several times last night, each one causing Max to react in such a strong way.

"Mmm."

His hand dipped around my navel, and the pads of his fingers tickled my skin as he moved toward my pussy. When he reached it, the gentleness was gone, and he rubbed my clit with a pressure that would easily make me come.

"I have thirty minutes until I have to get in the shower." His cock was slipping down my ass, pushing between my legs as I widened them.

He flirted with my entrance.

And, the more he teased, the wetter I got.

Within a few swipes, he was in, crown deep.

"That cock..."

"You fucking love it," he growled into the back of my ear.

He sank all the way in, and I released a shuddering breath, tingles bursting through my whole body.

"I do."

SIX
MAX

TALIA'S PUBLICIST, one of the forty employed by The Agency, had taken the red-eye to LA to meet with us this morning. Between the two of us, we were going to come up with a statement that would announce Talia's departure from the label. It was imperative that this was handled properly in the press. Something as petty as a false fucking rumor could ruin her reputation.

I wasn't going to let that happen.

So, the plan was for the three of us to meet at The Agency's condo in downtown LA. Once the statement was drafted, it would be released to the public. Talia's old label would then immediately respond with their own press release, and all the gossip would be squashed before it had a chance to fuel.

Now, the ladies were just waiting for me to show up, so we could get started.

Several minutes ago, the doorman had called to let me know they'd arrived. Since it would be a good fifteen minutes before I got there, I'd told him to escort the girls upstairs and make sure they were comfortable.

While I was logging into my email to see if Talia's publicist had sent me anything yet, my phone rang.

"Brett," I said as I answered.

"Disappeared a little early last night, didn't you?"

"I had some business to take care of."

I glanced out the window at the skyline of the city, thinking of the night I'd spent with Eve and the blonde. Eve had been so fucking naughty, but the two of them together had been epic.

"I saw." He laughed. "How was Lorrie?"

"Who?"

"Fucking Christ, Max. The girl who was tailing you on your way out."

"How do you know her?"

There was honking in the background, Brett spewing a mouthful to some fucker who had cut him off, before he said to me, "She's James's makeup artist. Don't tell me you never got her name."

"If she said it, I wasn't listening."

He laughed again, this time even louder. "Only you could get away with that shit."

"Don't even start, asshole. Before James tied you down, you were guilty of the same. Except, when you had threesomes, you didn't know either of the girls' names."

"Jesus, that seems like a lifetime ago."

"You make the engagement period sound real fucking fun."

"Man, you know what isn't fun? The weeks that pass when I'm not with my girl. Having her so far away from me all the time. When Jack is away from Samantha, he complains about it, too. You're the only one who doesn't."

"You two bitch like little girls."

He sighed. "Listen, motherfucker, I'm headed to Malibu for dinner tonight to meet with a few of the agents we used to work with. I want you to come."

"Recruiting?"

"Hell yeah. They'd be perfect for our LA office."

We were in the process of building one here that would be opening in the next few months. Scarlett and her team had been traveling back and forth for weeks to hire agents and publicists. Whenever Jack, Brett, or I were in town, if we had time, we'd also do some interviewing.

"Let me check if I'm free," I said, tapping the screen of my phone to pull up my schedule.

Talia was on my calendar until eleven, and then I was having lunch with a potential client. I had nothing else planned, so I was just going to go back to Eve's and get some work done until my early flight in the morning.

That reminded me, I still hadn't texted my ex back about lunch.

But there was no way I could fit her in.

"Pick me up at Eve's," I told him. "We'll drive there together."

"I'll see you then."

I slid the phone into my pocket just as the driver pulled up to the front entrance of the high-rise. The doorman approached the SUV and opened the backseat door for me. I slipped out and walked into the lobby toward the elevator. Once I was inside, I hit the PH button and leaned my back against the wall.

When I arrived on the top floor, the door slid across, revealing the foyer of our condo. The two women sat several feet away from me on the couch with coffee mugs in their hands.

"Max," they both said in unison.

I hugged each of the women, and then I took a seat on the chair across from them. "Let's not waste any time."

As the publicist nodded, she held a pad of paper on her lap and a pen in her hand.

She was ready.

I liked that.

"I want our message to be clear, and I want it to be simple. No celebrity alerts this time. If one of those notifications goes viral, we're in jeopardy of fucking everything up. We need this statement to go out and the label to come back with a response, and then we need to put this shit to bed."

"I want nothing more," Talia replied.

I looked at the publicist and said, "You know the contract Talia has waiting for her in Nashville is one of the biggest in country music history. Nothing is going to ruin that. Do you hear me?"

"I've got this handled, Mr. Graham. Don't worry."

I would believe that once this was over.

"Where do we stand on the press release? Has anything been written, or do we need to start from scratch?" I asked.

"I drafted two versions during the flight." Her laptop was resting beside her, and she opened it, her fingers tapping the keyboard. "I'm emailing you both options right now."

While she did, my eyes shifted over to Talia. "Did the label reach out to you last night after you got home?"

"A few unknown numbers came through my phone, but I didn't answer any of the calls. I've stayed off social media, and I didn't talk to any of my friends or my family, just like you asked."

"Good," I said, standing and going into the kitchen to grab myself some coffee.

While I waited for the single cup to brew, I flipped through the messages on my phone. Seeing the headlines of each one, realizing none of them needed my immediate attention, I clicked on my photos.

The first one that loaded was a picture of Eve that I'd taken this morning. Her foot was resting on the bathroom counter, and she was rubbing lotion onto her leg. The way the light was hitting her, the way her skin shone, the way her wet hair hung over her back and the side of her tit had made it a moment that had to be captured.

Damn it, she was one beautiful girl.

Seeing the time on the microwave, I knew her doorbell would be ringing any second. In the meantime, I had something else to give her. So, I clicked on the arrow at the bottom of the screen, attaching the photo to a text that I addressed to Eve. Underneath the picture I typed, *Gorgeous*, before I hit Send.

"The press releases should be in your inbox now," the publicist said.

I looked up from my phone, meeting her eyes, and then I glanced back at the picture.

Mmm.

I exited out of the text I had sent her, and I clicked on my email.

She was right; they were both there.

I took the coffee mug into the living room, set my phone next to it on the table, and said, "It's time to get to work."

SEVEN
EVE

ONCE MAX LEFT MY HOUSE, I threw on a pair of yoga pants and a tank top and sat in the middle of the living room floor. It was the only open spot since the couch was covered in shoeboxes.

God, this place was a mess.

Because of all my traveling lately, it had gotten completely out of control.

The hundreds of dresses I had in here had to be sorted and labeled, and accessories needed to be categorized. All of it then had to be put into garment bags and dropped off at my clients' houses. And I couldn't put it off any longer; it had to be tackled today while I had the time off.

I uncrossed my legs over the hardwood floor, and the shift caused me to feel the soreness in my ass. It was a dull ache but an extremely sweet one.

It reminded me of the pounding Max had given me last night and the one this morning.

A pounding I had begged for.

A pounding I wanted again right now.

That man.

And his magnificent cock.

I shook my head, trying to push out those thoughts, and hauled myself up off the floor. Just as I got to my feet, the doorbell rang. I answered it, and there was a man in a suit standing outside with an extremely large Hermès bag in his hand.

"Miss Kennedy?"

I nodded and backed it up with, "Yes." As the word left my mouth, I looked toward the curb and saw a black SUV was parked there.

"I have a delivery for you." He extended his hand in my direction.

I clasped my fingers around the handle of the bag and watched him leave my front steps before I closed the door. Since the only open space was the counter in the kitchen, I set the bag on top of it, admiring the gorgeous orange wrapping.

Hermès wasn't a company whose showroom I pulled from. Many of my clients collected their bags, and I would get them whichever ones they wanted to purchase, but they weren't worn on the red carpet. And, because I hadn't ordered any of their pieces recently, I couldn't imagine why I had gotten this delivery.

Inside was a box, typical of what their larger purses came in. I lifted the lid, and sitting on top of the dust bag was an envelope. I ran my finger under the flap, took out the card, and read the handwritten note.

Some things remind me of you.
This is one.
—Max

My hands began to shake as I reached into the box, opening the top of the dust bag to take out whatever was inside.

By the shape, feel, and weight, I knew it was a bag.

I just didn't know what collection he had gotten.

That was, until the handle slowly started to peek out.

"Oh my God!" I screamed, the dust bag falling to the ground as I held the purse into the air.

He'd bought me a fucking Birkin.

It wasn't the standard version, the one I got for most of my clients, which still had a waiting list that was several months long.

This was the Himalaya, made of dyed albino crocodile skin.

A rarity since only a limited quantity was produced.

One that was almost impossible to find.

It was the most breathtaking, stunningly beautiful bag I had ever seen.

And it was all mine.

I heard a text come through my phone from somewhere out in the living room.

I ignored it.

I couldn't move.

I couldn't put this baby down.

I certainly couldn't take my eyes off of it.

I ran my hand over the side and across the handle and under the bottom. It was so smooth, so silky, so lush.

I knew how much these bags went for, so I knew he'd spent a small fortune on it.

A fortune that was worth more than my car.

I glanced at the card again, reading the message he had written.

This masterpiece reminds him of me?

I felt my skin flush. A heat then began to spread to my heart and trickle through my chest.

More.

That was a word I'd been thinking about since my conversation with James.

I wasn't sure what that would look like.

If *more* meant additional bags like the one I was holding and like all the other expensive gifts he'd splurged on in the past...

If it meant spending more mornings waking up next to him and having more dinners together...

If my address would become the same as his...

But I didn't hate the way *more* sounded when I said it out loud.

I just didn't know the logistics.

There was no way I could move to Miami. Almost all of my business was in LA. However, The Agency was building an office here. Whenever I brought that up, Max would tell me they were still in the process of looking for someone to run it, and it wouldn't be Brett, Jack, or him.

So, even if I wanted more, I didn't know how to make that happen.

I set the bag on the counter, taking a few steps back, staring at the way the light hit the material.

I didn't know how I would ever thank him for this. I just knew I had to try.

I went into the living room, searching for my phone, positive it was somewhere in there. I found it on the floor where I'd been sitting before, and I tapped the screen, seeing that the text that had come in was from Max.

I hadn't expected to hear from him this early.

When I opened his message, there was a picture of me. I hadn't even realized he'd taken it. I'd been too busy putting lotion on after our shower. But I remembered several seconds of silence had passed between us when I saw that he was on the phone. I'd assumed he was checking his email. Never had I thought he was taking a photo of me.

Max: Gorgeous.

Tingles were already bursting through my body from the gift that was sitting in my kitchen. But, now that I had seen the picture of me and the word he had typed beneath it, the feeling had intensified.

I read his text a second, third, and fourth time.

First, the bag.

Now, this.

For a man who was always so dominating, a side I usually found the most attractive, his softness was proving to be just as sexy.

I clicked on the text box, and I began my reply.

Me: I don't even know what to say. Thank you certainly isn't enough.

Max: I got to be inside you last night and again this morning. I got to look at your body completely fucking naked. I should be the one thanking you.

Me: But the bag, Max. It's so beautiful. I'm speechless. I've never owned a piece of art as special as that one. And I'm certain nothing will ever top it.

Max: I'm glad you like it.

Me: I don't know how to show you how much I appreciate it, but I'll think of something.

Max: I know how...

Me: Oh, yeah?

Max: Come here. Right now.

Me: Where's here?

Max: The condo.

As I thought about his cock thrusting inside me, the tingles in my chest blasted down to my stomach, and they went straight to my clit. My body began to buzz.

Wetness lined the lips of my pussy.

I was so turned on.

Going to meet him would be as much for him as it would be for me.

Me: I'll be there in an hour.
Max: You have forty-five minutes.

He was such a hard-ass.

That was one of the things I loved about him.

But, even though the morning traffic rush was over, it would still take me a good thirty minutes to get to downtown, and before I left, I needed to get dressed and fix myself up a bit.

Me: I need more time than that.
Max: Forty minutes.
Me: You're relentless.
Max: Thirty-five.
Max: And I promise you'll say that again when I'm inside your pussy.

The tingles turned to a sharp pulse that was fluttering inside my clit.

I was throbbing for this man.

I squeezed my thighs together, trying to alleviate the sensation. But it didn't matter what I did because it wouldn't be enough.

I needed him.

His fingers.

His mouth.

His cock that I constantly dreamed about.

Me: I'll text you when I'm outside.
Max: Leave your panties in the car.

EIGHT
MAX

"THE STATEMENT HAS BEEN RELEASED," Talia's publicist said, slowly looking up from her laptop. "I sent it to every media outlet that's on The Agency's master list, and I posted it on all of Talia's social media pages."

"How long until her old label issues a reply?" I asked.

"An hour. Maybe less."

I stared at the screen of my phone, knowing, at any minute, a celebrity alert would come across it. That website was always the first to report news because they had more sources than any other publication in the world.

In this case, we'd sent the information to them directly.

Less than fifteen seconds later, my phone lit up.

BREAKING NEWS:

Talia Sweeny must be on to bigger and better representation now that she's cut ties with her label.

Wonder who's after the ex-reality star.

Or...who isn't.

Jesus, wasn't that shit the truth? I couldn't think of a single celebrity who hadn't tried to fuck her.

And, now that she was getting into country, changing her look, really playing up her innocent vibe, the guys would become even more obsessed.

Talia was a good girl. She didn't fuck around. She didn't date.

That made the men want her even more.

I told her that during many of our meetings. Being her agent, in an environment like the one we lived in, discussing her personal life was necessary because every goddamn thing could turn into a scandal.

But knowing how much she was wanted didn't faze her at all. She was focused on her career, on keeping her name untarnished, on building a brand that would set her up for life.

If only my other clients could do the same, that would save me a lot of fucking headaches.

"Well, it's not as bad as it could be," her publicist said, holding her phone in the air so that Talia and I could see she was referring to the celebrity alert. "They tend to be the harshest, and this one isn't."

She was right about that.

Before Eve, several alerts had gone out about me regarding the actresses I'd slept with. None of them had been pretty.

"Releasing a statement as quickly as we did put us in a better position," I told them just as my phone vibrated in my hand. "Had we waited, allowing the label to air their statement first, the result might not have been as good."

I looked down and saw the message was from Eve.

Eve: I just parked.

I stood and took off my jacket, setting it across the back of the chair. I then slid my phone into my pocket and moved to the far side of the living room, facing both women. "Listen, I've got to run out for a little while. I'll be back before the label issues their reply." I turned around and walked toward the elevator.

"If any of the media reaches out—and I'm sure they will—do you want me to say anything specific?" her publicist asked.

"Tell them you have no comment." I hit the button for the elevator and looked over my shoulder, catching Talia's eyes. "I want you off-line until tomorrow. By then, the news will have died down a little, and you can post a selfie or something. Make the message inspirational."

"Okay, I will," Talia replied.

The bell chimed, and I walked inside. Both ladies stared at me as the door closed.

I'd be gone twenty minutes, not a second more.

They'd be fine in my absence.

Talia's publicist was one of the sharpest on our team. She could handle any crisis that was thrown at her. With me, she just didn't take control, but that didn't mean she wasn't capable. She just knew that control wasn't something that I was ever willing to give up.

And, no matter what, that wouldn't ever change.

When I reached the main level, I came out of the short hallway where the private elevator was located, and I went into the lobby. As I made my way toward the front, Eve was approaching the building.

"Let her in," I said to the doorman, and he opened the door for her.

Eve was in a long dress that hung low on her chest. The fabric only covered the outer side of her tits, the material so thin that I could see the hardness of her nipples.

They looked so fucking good.

Christ.

I needed those nipples in my mouth, getting flicked with the tip of my tongue before I bit them between my teeth.

"Hi," she said as she reached me.

I clenched her hand within mine and led her back the way I had just come.

I said nothing as I brought her inside the elevator, pressing the PH button. Once the door closed and we began to climb, I waited a few seconds before I hit Stop.

"What are you—"

I wrapped my hands around the back of her head, cutting her off, and I brought her mouth to mine, preventing her from saying another word.

I didn't want to talk.

I didn't want to listen.

I just wanted to taste her.

So, I did, and the flavor that filled my mouth was fucking delicious. She was sweet like candy, her tongue hot, just like her cunt had been this morning.

I reached down and cupped her ass with both hands. That was when I realized she didn't have any panties on.

She'd listened to my order.

She was such a good fucking girl.

I lifted her, pushing her back against the wall as her legs wrapped around me. Once I had her settled, I reached underneath her dress and pressed on her clit.

"*Ahhh*!" she gasped

She was soaked.

Just how I wanted her to be.

I moved my palm to the top of her pussy while two of my fingers plunged inside her. As I rubbed her clit, I finger-fucked her in and out.

"Max..." she groaned, moans filling each breath.

"Hold on to me."

I waited for her to cling her legs even tighter around my waist, for her arms to circle my neck. Once both were secure, my teeth latched on to her bottom lip, and I kept them there, gnawing, as my free hand went to my belt. I unhooked it and then undid the button and fly, my suit pants dropping to my ankles. I lifted my cock out of my boxer briefs, removed my hand from her pussy, and put my tip there instead.

"Fuck *yesss*," she hissed as I pushed into her wetness.

So goddamn tight.

So warm.

So fucking wet.

"That cock," she purred when I was fully inside her.

I tilted my hips back and plunged in, holding the bottom of her thighs as leverage. I was fucking her so hard, the back of her head hit the elevator wall, her body sliding up and down against it.

If it hurt, she didn't tell me to stop.

What she did say was, "Faster."

So, I listened, and I reared back and sank forward and devoured her goddamn lips.

I knew she was close when her pussy began to contract.

"Come," I demanded, and I gave her the relentless fucking I had promised, knowing that would send her over the edge.

I was right.

Within a few strokes, she was screaming, her body shuddering against mine.

Not knowing if anyone could hear her, but not wanting to take the chance, I spread my lips over hers, and I swallowed her shouting.

While each of her breaths went down my throat, her cunt clenched my dick, and her wetness exploded over my skin.

The mix of the three felt fucking amazing.

When she finally stopped quivering, she said, "Oh my God,"

in a voice that was raspy from all the screaming. "You are incredible."

Her body was sensitive. It always was after she came.

That didn't mean I was going to be easy on her.

In fact, just the opposite was true.

My cock hammered into her even harder, my speed doubled, and I used every bit of power I had left.

By the way her pussy was milking my cock, I could feel that she was going to come again.

It was going to happen fast.

And I was right behind her.

My dick fucking pulsed, throbbing in pleasure, the build working its way through my balls and into my shaft, and I groaned, "Fuck," against her mouth.

She rocked her hips back and forth, taking control, owning the movements, squeezing each stream of cum out of me.

"Damn it," I roared, my fingers digging into her ass. "Your fucking pussy feels so good."

Her cunt then clamped around my dick, telling me we were getting off at the same time.

"Max!" she shouted, our lips glued, our tongues touching. "Ah!"

When she completely emptied me, her hips no longer bucking and her body still, she kept me buried in her snugness. Her hands then went to my face, and she pulled her mouth back, so her lips were barely touching mine.

It was slow.

Soft.

A kiss that wasn't full of hunger but still so fucking sexy.

Eventually, she put several inches between us and said, "Are we going upstairs?"

I shook my head. "I have a client up there and her publicist."

"Oh." She paused. "They're waiting for you?"

"Yes."

"At least I'll see you later tonight." She brushed her thumb over my lip, and I kissed it. "Do you want to order dinner in or go out and grab something?"

"I can't do either. Brett's picking me up, and we're going to Malibu for a work thing."

There was a change in her eyes.

It happened instantly.

It wasn't a look I had seen on her before, so I didn't recognize it. But it washed across her whole face, and then she began to wiggle as she tried to get out of my hold.

I growled, digging my fingers even deeper into her ass. "Don't move."

"I'm sure you have to get going."

"Kiss me."

"Max—"

"Fucking kiss me."

When her lips pressed against mine, they felt nothing like what I'd gotten from her earlier. They were hard, and her mouth was cold; it didn't even feel like she was breathing. They only stayed on me for a few seconds, and then her legs dropped from my waist, and her pussy slowly pushed me out until I felt the freezing air close around my tip.

Once she was standing, I tucked my cock back into my boxers and lifted my pants, zipping my shit up tightly and aligning my shirt so that it didn't look like I'd just fucked.

Now that I was ready and the bottom of Eve's dress was resting on the floor, I hit Stop and L, and that resumed the movement of the elevator, taking us back down to the main level.

The door opened, and Eve started to walk out.

I clasped her wrist, halting her before she turned the corner. She looked across her arm, the one I was holding, and I moved forward to kiss her again. Using my other hand, I held the back of her head, and my lips slammed against hers.

"I'll see you after. It shouldn't be too late."

She nodded, her body so tight, that strange expression still filling her eyes.

When I released her, she instantly turned into the hallway and disappeared from my sight.

I then took the elevator up to the condo. When the door swung open, the girls were on the couch in the same spots I'd left them.

They stopped their conversation and looked toward me while I said, "Did anything happen?"

"Lots of questions came in," the publicist said.

"And your response?"

"No comment."

I had known she could handle this.

I went to the fridge and grabbed a water, chugging half of the bottle before I took a seat in the chair. I pulled out my phone, the screen showing I'd been gone for seventeen minutes.

She'd gotten off twice, and I still had three minutes to spare.

The publicist's cell dinged, and she looked at whatever message had just come in. "The label released their statement."

"And?"

She was quiet for several seconds, as she seemed to be reading the screen. Then, she slowly looked up, and our eyes connected. "You were right. Releasing our statement first gave us the upper hand."

"Oh, thank God," Talia sighed.

I smiled and downed the rest of my water.

I had known today would be a good fucking day.

NINE
MAX

Kristin: I've been gone for three years, and not a thing has changed.
Me: LA is still the armpit of fucking hell. I told you that at the bar.
Kristin: I meant with you.
Me: Oh, yeah?
Kristin: Back then, you sucked at returning my calls and texts, and you still haven't improved. Since we're past lunch, how about dinner?
Me: I need a rain check.
Kristin: You're leaving in the morning?
Me: Yes.
Kristin: When are you coming back?
Me: I don't know.
Kristin: Then, I'll come your way. I have some friends I've wanted to visit in Miami, so it's the perfect excuse to see you both. I'll text you after I book my flight.
Kristin: I know I mentioned this last night, but it really was great running into you. You've done so good for yourself, Max. I always knew you would.
Me: I'll see you soon.

"WHAT A FUCKING MEETING," Brett said as the valet attendant pulled up his car, and we climbed into the front seat. He shifted into first and turned onto the road, heading back toward LA.

"Three more agents signed." I took out my phone and sent a quick text to Jack and Scarlett to let them know. "Where does that leave us? About forty more to go?"

"Something like that. Plus, we still have to find someone to manage it. Scarlett's been working like hell to find a good one."

The LA office wasn't going to be as big as our Miami one. At least, not right now. Still, we were going to have over eighty agents within the acting, music, and sports divisions and a full PR team. We just needed someone to oversee the place when the four of us weren't there.

Since Scarlett had been interviewing candidates, I'd been thinking about agents in Miami who we could promote to do it.

"What about Josh Martin?" I asked Brett, referring to one of our top acting agents. "He's been in the industry for a long time. He's proven himself over the years. He could handle doing it."

"I already thought of him, and Scarlett shot down the idea."

I glanced toward Brett. "Why?"

"His baby mama lives in LA."

"So?"

"I guess things ended badly, and living on opposite ends of the country is the only thing that keeps them from killing each other."

I laughed. "Fuck."

"Scarlett takes notes on all those bastards. Files that are inches thick."

This was news to me, although I wasn't surprised. Scarlett seemed to have dirt on everyone, and she used it to her advantage.

Unfortunately, that was also why her last relationship with Vince Hedman, Miami's quarterback, hadn't worked out.

However, she was the only person I knew who had starred in a celebrity alert and gotten that alert retracted. In its place, a few hours later, was a written apology from the owner of the company and a verbal promise that her name would never appear on their site again.

"I'm scared to know how thick my folder is," I said, still laughing.

We stopped at a red light, and he glanced at me. "She doesn't need files on us." He pointed at his head. "She's got that shit stored up here."

Now, we were both laughing.

"You're not going to believe who I saw before James's premiere." I sighed. "Kristin fucking Evans."

He looked at me again before he shifted. "You're shitting me. Is that why you were so late?"

"She's been working in Brazil for the last three years, and she just got back. I wanted to see how she was doing."

"What does she look like now?"

I turned my head toward the window, thinking about that night at the bar.

Kristin had always been a pretty girl. Athletic. High-maintenance. Determined like hell to get what she wanted. And, man, could she fucking cook.

I'd never tasted food like hers or seen anyone have such passion in the kitchen. The first time I had seen her in one, I had known she'd make the most perfect chef. After graduating from culinary school, she had become one.

Now that she was back in the States, restaurants in LA were fighting for she. She'd told me she hadn't yet decided which one she was going to pick.

"The same," I said. "Maybe even a little better."

He shook his head. "I remember all those nights she slept over in that first apartment we shared with Jack and Scarlett, right out of college. We didn't have real beds, just mattresses on the floor, and we took turns sleeping in the one bedroom and the living room. You and Kristin would be fucking, thinking you were being so quiet, but you were loud as hell, and the rest of us were trying to sleep through it."

"Those were some good times." I watched Brett pull into the left lane, trying to pass some of the slower traffic. "Just call it payback for all the girls you fucked in college on the bunk bed above mine."

"You mean, you weren't sleeping?"

"My fucking bed was shaking. Who could sleep through that?"

I thought about what I'd just said, and in unison, "Jack," came out of both our mouths, followed by the loudest laughs.

"So, what's up with Kristin? Are you going to see her again?" he asked.

I saw the skyline of LA peek into the distance, and I knew we weren't far from Eve's place.

"She's going to Miami to see some friends, and we'll probably get together."

"Are you going to tell Eve?"

I shrugged. "I haven't really thought about it."

"You're kidding."

"Not even close."

"Would you want her to tell you if she were hanging out with her ex?"

I didn't reply for several seconds, and then I said, "I don't know." I paused again. "I wouldn't expect her to. She does her thing; I do mine. It works for us."

"For you, but does it work for her?"

I nodded. "Yeah, I think so."

"Max, you guys have been playing this game for a long time, don't you think? Those trips to Miami she makes every few weeks are going to get old, and she's going to get tired of doing it. And, one day, she's going to want to get married, and where are you going to be with all that?"

I sucked in a breath and held it in.

Married?

Nah, I'd almost done that once.

I wasn't ever getting that close again.

"Who says Eve wants to get married?" I asked him.

"She's a fucking woman. That's what they all want."

I wiped my palms on my suit pants. "Damn."

"You have to know it's coming."

Is that true?

I tried to think of a sign that I'd missed or something she had hinted at.

I couldn't come up with anything.

"Brett, Eve and I are all about our jobs. Those come first, and they always have. She's never once brought up marriage or kids or any of that shit."

"But her best friend is getting married, and she's the maid of honor. I promise you, brother, the thought has run through her head."

"If it has, I don't want to hear about it." I waited a second to see if I felt any different. I didn't. "We're happy. We have a good thing going. She comes to see me when she's free. I see her when I'm doing business in LA. There's no reason to change that."

I felt him staring at me when he said, "You're not going to want to spend more time with her at any point?" I didn't answer, so he continued, "James and I are going to be married, and kids are in our future. Jack and Samantha are probably going to pop out another one as soon as they get married. Where does that leave you? Single for the rest of your life?"

"Dude, don't be fucking jealous. What I have sounds a lot easier than all that shit you're spelling out."

He came to another red light, and when the car stopped, he gripped my shoulder. "You and your fucking fist—one happy couple."

I punched the hand he was squeezing me with. "My fist is much cheaper than a divorce."

His hand went back to the gearshift, and we began to move again.

"In six months, you're going to tell me that Eve sat you down and had a conversation about the two of you spending more time together. Guess what I'm going to say?"

We were two years in, and we hadn't had that talk yet.

But the look I'd seen on her face in the elevator had been haunting me all fucking day.

I didn't like it.

And I didn't like that I wasn't sure what it had meant.

"I don't know what I'll do if that happens," I said.

"Listen, Max, I don't know much about relationships, but soon after James and I started dating, I knew I wanted her to live with me. I wanted to spend as much time with her as possible. And I wanted to make her mine."

Eve couldn't live with me when all her work was in LA, and I couldn't give her any more time than we already spent together.

We were exclusive.

She was mine.

Those two things were more than any girl who came after Kristin had gotten out of me.

She had it all.

Why would we want more?

TEN
EVE

I WAS SOAKING in the bathtub with a glass of wine and an overflowing mountain of bubbles when I heard Max open my front door.

Since James was tied up with movie stuff tonight, I figured I'd come in here to relax and calm my nerves and then get a few hours of sleep before he woke me with his mouth.

I still felt the sting of not being able to have dinner with him. Thinking I would get that much time had just been stupid.

But I had.

And it hurt.

However, I hadn't expected him to get back here this early.

I used my toes to turn off the water now that I'd let in a couple of inches of warmth to replace the cold I'd drained out. As I heard his shoes move across the floor, the sound getting louder the closer he got, I pushed my back against the porcelain tub. My fingers tightened around the glass, and I brought it to my lips. The sauvignon blanc burned the back of my throat as I swallowed several gulps.

"Damn, you're gorgeous," he said as he stood in the doorway. He leaned into the doorframe and crossed his arms.

His presence was like a fog that misted through the entire bathroom and thickened when it reached me.

"Hi," I whispered, taking in the dark navy of his suit.

He had close to a hundred in his closet in Miami.

I always favored this color because of the way it complemented his eyes.

They were so sharp. Piercing. And they were focused solely on me.

"I'm going to grab a drink and join you."

Before I had a chance to respond, he was gone, the sound of his shoes telling me he was moving toward the kitchen.

I could still feel him as though his hands were on my body.

It was always that way whenever he was near.

I had the strongest reaction to him. And the tingling he caused wasn't just in my pussy. It was in my chest, my stomach. It forced thoughts to fill my head.

Thoughts that hadn't necessarily made sense in the past, but my conversation with James had changed that.

More.

God, I wanted this man.

I heard the bottles rattle in the door as he opened the fridge and asked, "Do you want a refill?"

"Please."

There were new sounds—a cupboard opening, a glass being placed on the countertop. As I listened to him, anticipating his return, sweat began to drip down my neck. Each bead passed my chest, ran between my breasts, and disappeared into the water. I watched its path, my nipples growing hard, my legs pressing together to dull the ache between them.

My eyes finally lifted when he was standing in front of me.

I wrapped my fingers around his to take the wine from his

hand. He held on for a few extra seconds, the look on his face telling me how hungry he was. The intensity of his stare caused my clit to throb.

In those few moments, I felt so incredibly desired.

I knew that feeling would only grow once he was in the water with me.

Each layer he stripped from his body was set to the side of the sink. His shoes were left on the floor, his socks were next, and then he turned to face me.

Completely naked.

The candles that flickered around the back of the tub created the most romantic glow. They also gave just enough light that I could see his tan skin, the ripple of his abs, the tightness of his chest, and the small, dark patch of hair that covered it.

He wasn't like the actors I styled.

He wasn't primped and waxed and lasered and injected with every kind of filler.

He was all man.

And that was exactly the way I wanted him.

He put both feet in the tub and moved in behind me, sliding down until he was seated and his legs were surrounding mine. "Mmm," he growled as my back rested against his chest. "You feel so good."

So did he.

Hard and hot, and every inch of his skin that rubbed onto mine sent a shiver through me.

Holding the new glass of wine, I brought it to my lips and took a sip. "How was your work thing?"

He dipped his hand into the water, and then he ran his wet fingertips down my arm, stopping at my wrist and then going as high as my shoulder. "Productive."

"Oh, yeah?"

"Brett and I were interviewing new agents for the LA office. We hired all three we had dinner with."

The office they were building was only twenty minutes from my house, so he'd brought me there several times to show me the progress. He'd also told me about some of the agents who would be working there. Since a few of my clients were signed with them, I knew The Agency was inheriting some serious talent.

He wet his fingers again before dipping them down my breast and circling my belly button. He continued to go lower, touching the top of my pussy, wedging between my lips.

"*Ahhh*," I groaned as he gave my clit a quick, sharp stroke.

Just one.

But one that vibrated through my whole stomach.

He crawled back to my neck, teasing the skin around my collarbone and the tops of my breasts. Then, he used his palm to trace circles across each of my nipples. His touch was light. Just enough to flick the hardness, for me to crave the pinching of his fingertips.

"Max..."

His mouth left my hair and moved to the back of my ear. "Do you want something?"

During one of the rotations around my tit, his palm lowered, and his thumb clipped my nipple.

My back arched, and I moaned out a, "Yes."

He steered the wine glass that I was holding toward my other breast, the coldness landing on my nipple.

"Oh God," I breathed as the freezing sensation passed through me.

He held it there but brushed it over the peak and to the other side, so I felt it everywhere.

Just as it began to warm a little, he said, "Set the glass on the edge of the tub, and put my hand where you want it."

I did the first part, and then I returned to his fingers, clasping mine around them. They were so long, manly, powerful. They needed to be between my legs.

So, that was where I put them.

And that was where I left them as I gripped the edge of the porcelain. "*Fuuuck*," I groaned as he flicked up and down my clit.

"Always so wet for me."

I knew there was a difference between my wetness and the bath water because, as his cock pressed against my lower back, I could feel the thickness of his pre-cum as several beads of it leaked out.

His fingers slithered up and down several times before he replaced them with his palm while those same fingers dived into me.

"*Yesss*," I panted. "That's what I want."

My legs spread, and water sloshed out the side of the tub. It happened again when my back slammed into his chest and the top of my head ground into his shoulder.

"I love this fucking pussy," he grunted. "So tight. So fucking perfect."

His palm glided across me, using the pressure I needed, and he fingered me with such a speed that a build immediately took over my body.

It happened fast.

And, as if he sensed it, he moved even quicker.

Harder.

Deeper.

And then I heard, "Come for me."

My nails found his thigh, and I dug them in as waves of pleasure spread over me.

"Mmm, that's what I want," he growled in my ear.

He pumped out each swell and slowed as the orgasm began to pass.

Once I stopped moving, he pulled his fingers out and trailed them up my pussy and in between my breasts. Then, he rested them on his lips. He sucked off whatever had dripped from them.

"That's not going to hold me off for long."

"What do you want?"

"My tongue on your cunt."

I sighed as the tingling returned.

His tongue was as talented as his cock.

And I loved both.

Equally.

"Finish this," I said, lifting his glass of scotch off the edge of the tub while grabbing mine, too. "Then, you can put your mouth wherever you want." My body was still so sensitive; I needed a second to recover. While he took a sip, I changed the subject and asked, "Did you go over to the new office today?"

"Didn't have time. I'm going to try to get over there before my flight in the morning."

"Has Scarlett hired anyone to run it yet?"

"Nah."

I smiled even though he really couldn't see it. "You know what that means, don't you?"

"What?"

I'd been thinking about this since we fucked in his elevator.

Brett wouldn't take the job. James loved Miami too much, and she'd made it her home. Jack's daughter, Lucy, was established in a private school, and it would be too hard for him and Samantha to relocate. Scarlett's entire finance team was at their headquarters, so it made no sense for her to go.

That left Max.

"You can't hand your baby off to a stranger and expect them to do as good of a job as you would. So, you should be the one to run the LA office."

I nuzzled my face into his chest, watching his profile, the way his beard moved when the muscles in his jaw flexed. How his tongue skimmed the inside of his lip.

If he lived here, I could do this much more often.

We could be together whenever one of us wasn't traveling.

I could have *more*.

"Nothing in this world would make me want to move back here," he said. "I fucking hate this town."

Nothing.

Not even me.

Before he had gotten in this tub, *more* had seemed so close.

Now, it was as far as LA was to Miami.

And I seemed to be the only one bothered by it.

His mouth moved to the side of my ear. "Stand up."

I swallowed hard, trying to hide the disappointment that was plaguing me. And, because I knew it was on my face, I tried to mask that as well. "I'm good right here."

"No," he said. "You're going to stand and turn around, and then you're going to put your pussy in my face, so I can eat it."

We had such little time together that I didn't want to fight.

But I also felt like I needed to say something.

"Eve," he growled in the back of my ear.

Here was the problem.

My heart was starting to want him as badly as my body.

ELEVEN
EVE

James: We're in the same state, finally, and I haven't seen you in almost 48 hours.
Me: Max's fault. You know I'm married to his peen whenever he's nearby. But he left this morning, so I'm free. Dinner?
James: You read my mind. Brett has another meeting tonight, so you can have me until at least midnight.
Me: Good. I need your ears.
James: What's going on?
Me: Adulting kinda stuff.

MY CELL STARTED TO RING, and James's name and a picture of the two of us appeared on the screen.

I laughed as I hit Accept and said, "Seriously? I'm going to see you tonight."

"You never bitch about adulting, which means whatever is bothering you has to do with Max, and you never bitch about him, so this has to be serious."

"You know me too well."

"Ugh, girl, if I wasn't driving to the studio right now, I'd be headed to your place with a case of wine. Tell me what's going on."

I backed away from the clothing rack I'd been organizing and took a seat on the couch. Since Max had left so early and I wasn't able to fall back asleep, I'd used the time to finish clearing it off.

At least I was productive in his absence.

I rested my elbows on my knees and said, "I've been thinking about the conversation we had the other day. You know, the whole me-ever-wanting-more-with-Max thing."

"And it pains you to admit that I'm right, but...I'm right."

"Maybe."

"I'm no expert, obviously. My history with men isn't exactly extensive, as you know. But I know my best friend, and lots of times, I know what you're going to do before you do it. And I know this flying-back-and-forth thing sucks because I do it and I hate it and I don't even commute as often as you do."

I chewed the corner of my thumbnail, pressing my other fingers against my temple. "I told Max last night that I thought he should oversee the LA office."

"Finally! What did he say?"

I knew his answer by heart.

I'd been hearing his response in my head since he said it.

I'd even heard it while he was licking my pussy in the bathtub.

And again while we had sex on the bathroom counter.

And when he kissed me good-bye this morning.

Over and over.

Like a damn woodpecker, gnawing at my nerves with each pound of its beak.

"He said, 'Nothing in this world would make me want to move back here. I fucking hate this town.'"

"Ugh. I know."

"You...*know*?" I stood and started pacing the living room,

stepping around the boxes of shoes that were propped against the wall and the racks of dresses and suits I had everywhere and the tower of sunglasses I'd just labeled this morning.

"While I was in Norway, Brett said that Scarlett was having a hard time with finding someone to run that office. I told Brett that Max should be the one to do it, and Brett said Max would never move back to LA. I guess all the partners have asked him, given that he's the most flexible, and he told all of them no."

What surprised me about this conversation was that everyone knew Max would never relocate here.

Everyone but me.

"This is so fucked up," I said, stopping at the entrance of the kitchen, seeing Max's coffee cup in the sink. "And it puts so much pressure on me."

"It does."

"But, James, I can't move to Miami permanently. My clients are here, and I've worked my ass off to get the ones I have."

"I know, babe."

I turned, pushing my back against the wall and sliding down until my ass hit the floor. "There has to be a solution that doesn't require me being the only one sacrificing. Because, as it stands right now, I'm the one who's constantly traveling to see him. It's rarely the other way around unless he comes here for work."

"You two are going to have to compromise."

I laughed even though nothing about this was funny. "We're talking about Max Graham. That man doesn't compromise. He's as ruthless in business as he is in the bedroom and everyday life. It's his way. Always. And there are no exceptions."

"My vag just applauded that statement. The rest of me got stabby."

I shook my head. "Now, you know why adulting is such a bitch."

"What I do know is that you've finally come to a conclusion.

That's a big step. So, now, we need to come up with a plan on how to get what you want."

"It's going to be nearly impossible."

"That's where you're wrong. You have something that Max wants, and that gives you the upper hand."

"What's that?"

"Your vagina."

TWELVE
MAX

Kristin: I arrive in Miami two weeks from tomorrow. I'm there for ten days. Think you can squeeze me in?
Me: I'm sure my PA can tweak my schedule to make it work.
Kristin: Great. Can't wait to see you again.

THE LABEL'S receptionist had seated Talia and me in the conference room. Since our meeting wasn't for another fifteen minutes, I should have been tackling the hundreds of emails that had come in over the last hour. Instead, the whole goddamn time I'd been here, I'd been texting Kristin.

And, now, I had a new text box open that was addressed to Eve, and my fingers were hovering above the screen.

I wasn't messaging her out of guilt.

I just missed the fucking girl.

Me: I wish my face were between your legs right now.
Eve: Good afternoon to you, too.
Me: I've been thinking about you since I got on the plane this morning.

Eve: Oh, yeah?
Me: Non-fucking-stop.
Eve: I hope the thoughts in your head involve you getting on the plane and coming back to LA.
Me: They involve your pussy and how many orgasms I'm going to give you.
Eve: But you're so far away...
Me: I won't be for long. You're coming to Miami soon.
Eve: I'm so swamped with work right now, Max. My clients need me for premieres and awards shows, so I have to stay in LA.
Me: You'll fly to Miami with Brett and James next Thursday, and you'll spend the weekend with me.
Eve: I can't.
Me: But you want to. I know you do. Because you miss me, and I miss you.
Eve: Why don't you come to LA to see me?
Me: I'll be there next month for the soft opening of The Agency, three weeks later for a meeting, and a month after that for the grand opening. It's your turn.
Eve: Fine.
Me: I'll change fine to fuck yes when I call you later tonight and get you to come for me on the phone.

The door opened, and I immediately shoved my phone into my pocket. Making sure Talia heard the noise as well, I took a quick glance over my shoulder to where she was seated, and she was tucking her cell into her bag.

Our eyes locked, and I saw the fear on her face.

She had nothing to worry about, but I understood where the concern came from.

This was the biggest meeting of her whole fucking life.

And, even though it was already in the bag, the contract hadn't been signed by either party.

It would be within the next hour.

I turned back toward the door, and an older man was walking through it, looking like he was coming off the set of a western. Black cowboy hat, denim shirt, bolo tie—everything I would expect from an old-timer in Nashville.

My eight-thousand-dollar custom Tom Ford suit certainly didn't fit in here.

"Edwin Parsons," the older man said as he approached me. "CEO of Old Country Records." He stopped a few feet away and held out his hand.

I'd anticipated the head of A&R since we'd spoken several times on the phone, and I suspected he was the man standing behind Edwin. I'd figured several label executives would be attending our meeting as well due to the size of Talia's contract. I assumed that was the team of four who walked in next. I just hadn't thought the CEO of the label would be meeting with us, too.

But I fucking liked it.

Big dogs didn't scare me.

I actually preferred to be in their presence.

I got on my feet and shook his hand. "Max Graham. It's a pleasure to meet you, Edwin."

"When I heard you were coming in, I cleared my schedule. It's not every day an artist changes genres and is offered the highest contract our company has ever written. I had to meet the man who was responsible for it."

"She's worth it," I told him.

"I believe she is indeed." He released my hand and looked at Talia, gripping her fingers much lighter than he had with mine. "Miss Sweeny, you're now our highest-paid recording artist ever to date. What do you think about that?"

"It's an honor, Mr. Parsons."

"We're happy to have you, dear, and we're anxious to see what you're going to bring to country music."

What Edwin wanted to say was that Talia had found herself a hell of an agent who had ridden the fuck out of them until he got what he wanted. And, now, the label was shitting their pants, worrying that Talia wouldn't sell enough albums to cover their ass.

Edwin didn't have to worry.

Talia would deliver.

And, when her contract with Old Country Records was up for renewal, I was going to reach out to all of their competitors and work them against each other to get her an even higher deal.

She was worth it.

So was I.

THIRTEEN
EVE

"WE'RE MAKING our final descent into Miami," the flight attendant whispered to Brett and me, so she wouldn't wake James, who was sleeping on the couch. "Is there anything I can get you?"

Brett held up his tumbler, signaling he'd like a refill.

"No, thank you," I said, and I immediately heard the sound of an email coming through my phone.

I lifted my cell off the table and held it in my hand, scrolling across the other messages that had come in with it.

While James had been sleeping for the last hour, I'd used that time to catch up on paperwork and billing and scanning some of the résumés that I'd saved on my laptop. I had finally realized I couldn't put it off any longer and had to hire an assistant. In the last week, I'd made an effort to find one.

But because I'd been so buried in work, I hadn't checked my email the whole flight. Lots of the messages were clients forwarding me their schedules, some were invitations to go visit new showrooms across the US, and several were from designers, encouraging me to attend their shows and check out their new lines.

And then there was the most recent email that had come through.

I pressed my thumb on the message, so it would take up the whole screen.

Miss Kennedy,
Allow me to formally introduce myself. I'm Alberto Romano, Chief Designer at Horse Feathers. I know you're well acquainted with our brand and that you have visited our Los Angeles showroom many times and have even dressed a few of your clients in our pieces. I'm aware that our CEO has reached out to you personally to thank you, and I would like to as well. We appreciate your trust in our company, and we're honored that you've given us a chance in a market that's already filled with established, highly talented designers.

Since our company was birthed three years ago, your name has constantly been mentioned among our design team. You're someone we've followed closely and watched as your business grew, and now, you're one of the most desired, sought-after stylists in the States. Based on your work and reputation, we understand why. Your taste is eclectic and timeless, and we believe there are so many things we can learn from someone as skilled and gifted as you.

My team and I are based in Milan, but we'd like to set up a meeting with you in the States to discuss the future of our company and how we see you involved in our upcoming plans. As I type this, our legal team is writing up a formal offer that I'll present to you when we meet. Hoping you're interested, I would ask you to please send me your schedule, and I'll have my assistant put together a travel itinerary.

I look forward to hearing from you.

Ciao,
Alberto

A formal offer?

I scanned the email again to make sure I'd read it correctly.

When I saw that I had, I repeated that line over and over in my head, trying to make sense of it.

What the hell?

Alberto didn't actually mean that he was offering me a job.

He couldn't have meant that.

As he'd said in his email, I was one of the most sought-after stylists; therefore, I barely had time to breathe, never mind consider having a second job.

But it did sound like he was coming all the way from Italy to meet with me.

And, because I was dying to know what this was all about, I'd definitely schedule a time to get together with his team, but there was no chance I'd do more than just listen.

I loved my gig, my clients, the trust they had in me, and the relationship I'd developed with designers.

I wouldn't give that up for anything.

Not even Max.

Sigh.

"Are we far?" James said as she lifted her head off the couch.

She looked down toward her feet where I was sitting, and I said, "Just a few more minutes."

Her eyes shifted over to Brett, and she smiled.

He returned the gesture and held out his glass in her direction. "Want some?"

She nodded and brought it to her lips.

"James," I said as I finished inputting the last of my clients' schedules into my calendar, "your assistant hasn't sent me anything for this week. You really don't have any events while you'll be in Miami?"

The partners always had something to attend in Florida. They could have something almost every night if they accepted all the invitations that came in. And she usually accepted at least one.

She glanced at Brett again. "Nope. He's keeping me chained up for the next four days."

I laughed. "In other words, I'll see you when you return to LA."

She gazed at me with the biggest grin on her face. "Not even close."

Something felt off.

"Do you feel like clarifying?" I asked.

James sat up and turned toward the large circle window, watching the plane lower as we quickly approached the city.

"You're seriously ignoring me right now?"

She continued to do so, so I sighed and turned my attention back to my phone. Now that I had my clients' schedules, I decided to reply to Alberto.

Hi Alberto,
It's so nice to hear from you. Thank you so much for your kind note.

I have enjoyed watching the growth of Horse Feathers. Your brand has come a long way, and my clients enjoy every time I dress them in one of your designs.

I'll be back in LA late next week, and I will be in town until the end of the month. Please feel free to pick a day that works best for you. With plenty of notice, I can make almost any of the dates work.

I look forward to meeting you.
—Eve

The plane landed, and as we moved toward the base of the private airport, I saw an SUV pull onto the runway. I knew it was the transportation that would be taking the three of us home.

This was the process, the journey I took every few weeks, whether I flew alone or with one of Max's partners.

I tossed my phone into my bag, my laptop was next, and I opened the bottle of water I'd been sipping earlier.

Knowing Max would be working all day tomorrow, I'd have plenty of time to finish the things I hadn't today. That meant I could set up some interviews for when I returned to LA, and I could reach out to a realtor and have them start looking for some office space. And, because Max never unplugged over the weekends, I knew I'd have several more opportunities to pull out my laptop and get some hours in.

I needed it.

Because, the second I got back to California, things were about to get extremely busy. I had over twenty clients to style for the upcoming week and a few more heading out on press tours where they'd need several weeks' worth of outfits.

Now that we were stopped, the flight attendant opened the main cabin door and released the staircase that dropped to the ground.

I grabbed my bag and stood.

Before I reached the front, Max entered the plane.

"Hi," I said, surprised to see him.

He never met me at the airport. I always waited for him at his house, and it could sometimes be hours before he got there.

He didn't respond.

He just walked up to me and put his hands on my cheeks and his mouth on mine.

Tingles burst through my entire body, and they settled inside my stomach.

It hadn't even been two weeks since he left LA.

I'd missed him so much.

My body, my heart—all of me.

As he kissed me, I closed my eyes and inhaled his cologne. It was the sexiest smell, especially when it was combined with the feel of his cock as it pressed against me. It was already hard, but the more his lips devoured mine, the longer it grew.

Knowing James and Brett could be watching, I didn't straddle his waist and grind my pussy against his dick.

But I wanted to.

Once he eventually pulled away, I heard the door behind him close, and the flight attendant approached us.

"Please let me know if I can get you anything, Mr. Graham," she said before she moved toward the back of the plane.

Get him anything?

"Are we going somewhere?" I asked him.

He took my hand and led me back to the couch I'd been sitting on. James was now next to Brett in the row of seats across from us, so Max sat beside me and said, "I'm getting you out of town."

Excitement began to mix with the tingles, and I glanced at James. "Are you guys coming, too?"

"Hell yeah, girl," she blurted out. "Bathing suits and maxi dresses for the next four days."

When James had asked me yesterday if I traveled with my passport, I hadn't thought much about it. Now, her question made perfect sense. The only problem was that I hadn't packed right for this trip. I only had one bikini with me. One dress. I didn't even think I'd grabbed a cover-up.

"I can tell by your face that you're freaking out a little," James said. "But I don't want you to worry. While you were in the shower the other day, I snuck around your house and grabbed everything that Max had instructed me to. It's all on the plane now. And, whatever I didn't get, he bought, so it would all be new for this trip."

"I seriously love your ass," I said. Then, I gazed at Max, and I felt my voice start to soften, a wave of emotion working its way through me. "Why?" I whispered to him.

"I knew you could use it, and if James could come, I had a feeling you'd have an even better time, so I worked it out with her and Brett. Jack and Samantha and Scarlett were tied up, or they would have also come."

He'd kept the trip a secret, coordinated all of our schedules, had James grab things around my house, and bought whatever she hadn't packed.

And he'd done all of this for me.

More.

I wrapped my arms around his neck and pressed my lips against his cheek. His beard was rough and scratchy, and I loved how it felt on my skin. What I loved even more was the feeling inside my chest.

"You did so much for me."

He nuzzled my face, causing his whiskers to scratch even harder. "You're worth it."

FOURTEEN
MAX

VACATION SEX.

It was my fucking favorite.

There was something about a bed full of pillows and all the extra counter space in the rooms and the glass walls of the shower and all the other surfaces that I'd gotten to fuck Eve on that I liked.

Shit, my dick got hard, as I just thought about it.

But that was only one of the reasons I enjoyed getting her out of town.

The other was that, when I took her somewhere tropical, she showed so much more of her body. Bikinis during the day, dresses at night. She never wore a bra or panties, so there was just one layer resting over her skin.

One thin, tiny layer that was separating us.

And I constantly broke that layer, my teeth nipping those hard fucking nipples, my fingers sliding into that warm, tight cunt.

I never had to wait to have her.

So, I'd taken advantage of that from the second the plane lifted into the air.

And I'd continued to taste her every few hours for the last three days.

Holding her body against mine, I ran the tip of my finger down the backside of her arm. She let out a long, deep breath, and I did it again.

Goose bumps rose over her body, and her legs swished over the sheets.

It was past eight in the morning. She never slept this late unless she was on island time. Here, she shifted into a slower pace. She didn't check her phone as often. She ate more and always ordered dessert.

She was even hotter when she was this relaxed.

But, from the second we'd landed in Punta Cana, I'd noticed something was distracting her. And, thinking back over the last several weeks, this wasn't the first time I'd felt it. I'd heard it in her voice, and more recently, I'd seen it in her face.

She was stressed.

I was sure that was it.

I decided not to push her for answers. That wasn't what this trip was about. I needed us to unplug, and my job was to make her as relaxed as possible.

My mouth was capable of that.

So, I rolled her onto her back and moved down her body, lifting the tiny piece of lace that hung to the top of her pussy. That was the only scrap of clothing I let her sleep in because it looked so fucking sexy on her. Situating myself between her legs, I felt her stir, but my attention was locked on the bare cunt that sat a few inches below me. Holding her open, I pressed my nose onto the middle of her clit.

And, slowly, I inhaled.

Fuck.

I could never get enough of that perfect smell. One that was so unique to Eve. One that I wanted to coat myself in.

I lifted my nose and stuck out my tongue and swiped it across the entire length of her clit.

"Max," she groaned, her hands fisting my hair, tugging it from the goddamn roots. "*Yesss.*"

She loved when I ate her pussy.

But there was no way she could love it as much as me.

That was why I spent so much time down here.

Why I thought about it every day she was away from me.

Why I made her show it to me when we video-chatted at night.

I kept my tongue at the top of her clit and slid two fingers inside her, licking at the same time I drove in and out of her pussy.

My cock was so fucking hard, growing from her sounds, from the way her hips bucked the air, from how good I was making her feel.

And I knew that because the walls of her pussy were clenching my fingers, telling me how close she was to coming.

I increased my speed and sucked her clit into my mouth, holding it between my teeth. As I rubbed my tongue across the edge, her back arched. So, I pumped my fingers, twisting them at the knuckles, and I felt her build.

"Oh God!" she screamed.

Mmm.

My teeth released her, and I just licked.

Licked as hard as I fucking could, and she immediately began to shudder.

"Max, yes!"

She let go of my hair, and her hands went to my shoulders, nails digging straight into me. Her thighs clenched my face, and my beard scratched them.

I knew that was what she was after.

She fucking loved the feel of my whiskers on her skin.

And, as she got more of it, she moaned even louder.

When her body eventually stilled, I gently lifted my mouth off of her and shifted onto my side, pulling her against my chest.

"I wish I could wake up this way every morning." She sighed.

"With my tongue?"

"Well, yes, but I meant just with you."

I growled against her cheek, my lips brushing over it before I asked, "Have you had a good time in Punta Cana?"

She nodded. "I always do when we travel together. The trips you plan are incredible."

I couldn't take much credit for any of the plans. My assistant had put together every trip we'd ever been on. But I always picked the destinations, and this time was no different.

For this long weekend, my assistant had gotten the four of us a six-bedroom house on the beach. It came fully stocked with butlers and maids and a chef. When Eve and James weren't spread across the sand or in the ocean, we would find them floating in the infinity pool.

She needed time with her best friend.

Time with me.

This trip had given her both.

But, once we got back to the States, I was going to be busy as fuck.

I didn't like that I'd be seeing so little of her.

I just had no other choice.

She ran her fingers through my hair and down my cheek. "I can't believe it's our last day here. It went by too fast."

"There will be other trips; you know that."

"For some reason, I feel like they won't be happening for a long time."

She was always so goddamn intuitive.

"Eve, I'm not going to lie; things are going to be pretty rough for a little while." I circled my thumb across her shoulder and went down to her chest and back up. "My schedule is fucking ugly."

"What does that mean?"

"I'll probably get to see you only once a month. That's all I can fit in."

Her eyes locked with mine. "How long is that going to last?"

"Three, possibly four months. It depends on if I meet my clients overseas, but right now, it's looking that way."

She looked surprised. She shouldn't have been. Toward the beginning of our relationship, we had gone almost the whole summer without seeing each other. That was the kind of business I was in.

She knew that.

As I reached for her face, she pulled back. Her body turned stiff, and the glare in her eyes was identical to when she'd walked out of the elevator after we fucked in it.

"Don't worry about this right now; we'll deal with it once we're home."

Her stare bounced between my eyes several times before she said, "Sounds like it's already been dealt with."

That fucking mouth.

My hand inched forward again. This time, she let me wrap it around her cheek. "Go get dressed, so we can grab some breakfast downstairs." My thumb dipped to her lip, and I gently tugged it. "Then, we'll take the Jet Ski's out."

"Fine, but I need you to give me a minute." Her tone was flat, her eyes almost defeated.

Some time with me on the water would fix that. I just needed to get her out there and get her mind off the news I'd just delivered, so I climbed out of bed and looked for a clean pair of swim trunks. When I found some, I slid them on and went into the bathroom.

"What time is our flight tomorrow?"

"Ten." I grabbed my toothbrush, squirted a line of toothpaste over it, and stuck it into my mouth.

"The plane will drop off you, Brett, and James in Miami, and then I'll continue on to LA?"

I moved to the doorway of the bathroom while I brushed, so I could see her. "Jack, Samantha, and Lucy will be flying with you. They're taking her to Disneyland."

"Oh, that's cute."

"They do everything for that kid."

She sat higher in bed, pulling the blanket up to her chest, hiding the lace that covered her tits. "You would, too, if Lucy were your child."

I took the toothbrush out of my mouth and shook my goddamn head. "I just don't know how Jack manages it all. I sure as hell couldn't."

"He makes time, Max, because he wants to. He'll have to again when they have their second child, which I'm sure will happen sometime soon."

I walked to the sink to spit, and when I was done, I looked at her and said, "This is why we work so well together, Eve, because neither of us would ever want something like that."

FIFTEEN
EVE

JAMES and I were standing in the shallow end of the pool with wine glasses in our hands. The sound of the ocean and the rustling of the palm trees were almost as loud as my thoughts.

After getting back from jet-skiing, the guys had gone inside to do some work, and James and I had found our way out here. That happened almost every day around this time. For a few hours, I would get to have my best friend all to myself, savoring these moments since I knew it would be weeks before I saw her again.

At least it wouldn't be a month.

Like Max.

That was complete bullshit, and so was his ridiculous work schedule.

I understood this was what I had signed up for, that he was in the prime of his career and that slowing down now would only send him backward.

My situation wasn't any different.

But that didn't mean I liked it or that the conversation we'd had this morning hadn't gutted me.

Because, as I waded in this pool, my chest feeling so tight and heavy, my heart was literally screaming, *More.*

I needed it.

And, God, I wanted it.

But the man I'd been dating for the last two years had told me he wouldn't be able to manage it all—me, work, us.

That wasn't even the worst of it.

The worst had come at the end of the conversation when he told me that we worked so well as a couple because a family wasn't anything either of us would ever want.

Marriage wasn't something we'd discussed before.

It certainly hadn't been the first thing on my mind when I met him two years ago on James's balcony.

And it was something I wouldn't have necessarily pushed for. I'd watched my parents get divorced when I was ten years old. I had seen what it did to our family. But, before that, I had seen how being wed had made them into two of the most miserable people.

I didn't want that.

I didn't want the possibility to be taken away from me either, especially because, over the time we'd been together, he'd grown to mean so much to me.

But, as for having kids, I still felt that punch in my stomach, the burn in the back of my throat, the unsteadiness it sent to my limbs.

Just because I didn't talk about having children didn't mean I didn't want them.

Whatever had caused him to assume this, he couldn't have been more wrong.

"Refills?" I heard someone say, sucking me out of my thoughts.

I turned my head and saw one of the butlers moving toward

the edge of the shallow end. He knelt to set down two glasses of cucumber water.

"I'm good," James said, "but please get her another and keep them coming."

As the butler disappeared to go get me more wine, I glanced at my best friend. "Are you trying to get me wasted?"

"You have a lot going on up there"—she nodded toward my head—"so I'm hoping it calms you down a little."

"You might be right."

"Girl, you've been so distracted since we got in this pool; you didn't hear any of the story that I was telling you before the butler showed up."

I felt my brows rise. "You were talking?"

She laughed. "I was going on and on. It doesn't matter. What matters is the thing that's eating you right now, so start talking."

I sighed as I walked to the side of the pool, pressing my shoulders against the hard stone and resting my arms over the brick pavers. I tilted my head back, the sun coming down hard, tingling my forehead. "I'm in a weird place with Max."

"I know, and we need to do something about it."

I lifted my head to look at her. "But how? I want more from my boyfriend—things that he won't ever give me. I want more from my job, and I already work twenty-four/seven. I basically want to be in two places at once—change Max's priorities and have everything I've ever wanted, all at the same time." Before she could respond, I added, "It's impossible. I know."

James swam several feet closer, and she put her arms on the edge of the pool to hold herself up. "You know I've been there before. God, I feel like I'm there at least once a month."

My body straightened. "But, James, it's not even close to the same thing. You and Brett make it work. You want to take your relationship to the next level. You want marriage and kids. Max and I..." My voice trailed off.

As I was about to reveal the conversation I'd had with him this morning, James said, "Eve, it's not easy. In fact, it's so much harder than I ever thought it would be. And, every month, I swear, it gets worse because the two of us keep getting busier." She turned, resting her side against the pool while she held her cheek with her palm. "It's going to take a lot of hard work, and the both of you are going to have to sacrifice, but you'll find a solution."

A memory from this morning flashed in my head. It was the look on Max's face when I'd told him that Jack had to make time for his family. It was as though the concept was completely foreign to him.

Like he couldn't fathom it.

Like he'd never even consider it.

"We'd both have to sacrifice; that's the only way it would be fair. But, based on some of the things he's said, I worry that it would just be me doing it," I told her.

"I don't believe that."

"It's true." My voice wasn't higher than a whisper.

The butler returned with my glass of wine, taking the half-full one that had warmed under the sun. Once he left, I wrapped my fingers around the chilly stem.

Sacrificing for Max would mean downsizing my business. Losing some of the fifty clients I had worked my ass off for. Hiring a staff larger than just the one I'd planned, so I wouldn't have to be in LA all the time. I'd have to give up my rental and the money I'd saved to go toward a down payment on my first real home would just have to be spent on something else.

Did he deserve all of that?

He had swooped into my life so fast. I'd almost immediately questioned everyone I'd dated in the past. I'd compared them all to Max, and they couldn't measure up. Not just physically—

although there was that, too. He owned my body; his devotion to it made me feel a pleasure I hadn't known was possible.

When it came to sex, Max Graham had no competition.

But, emotionally, there was a difference, too. It was intense. A surge that grabbed ahold of my heart and didn't let go. A pulsing in my chest that was so strong, I felt it in the back of my throat. A feeling of warmth that wasn't just on my skin.

But, after this morning, I'd learned I was the only one.

Even if I were willing to throw it all away, that wasn't what he wanted. He was happy where things were. And he was relieved I didn't want what Jack and Samantha had.

A family.

"You both will sacrifice," she said after a short pause. "It won't just be you."

I stared into her eyes, searching for the answer before I asked, "How are you so sure?"

"Because, if he doesn't, he's going to lose you."

My lungs tightened as I broke contact with James and looked out toward the ocean.

Now, it was my turn to address a thought that had been so foreign up until she said it.

A breakup.

Was that where our relationship was headed?

If only one of us was willing to meet in the middle, what other choice did we have?

But that would mean not having Max in my life.

A man I didn't want to live without.

A man I knew I loved.

Maybe I'd rather have a part of him than nothing at all.

SIXTEEN
MAX

Me: You free later? I'm going to video-chat you when I get home.
Eve: I'll be with a client until pretty late. You'll probably be asleep by the time I get out.
Me: I fucking miss you.
Eve: Me, too.

I STARED at Eve's last message for a few extra seconds, and then I dropped my phone onto my desk.

This week was supposed to be an easy one for her. So easy that she'd called a few days ago and asked if she could come to Miami tonight and tomorrow night to visit. While I had been on the phone with her, I'd checked my schedule and agreed.

But, when I had gotten to the office the next morning, my calendar had synced with the one my assistant maintained for me, and I had seen that both days and nights were filled.

I'd had to call Eve and tell her it wouldn't work, that I had too much going on with work and that it wouldn't be fair to bring her all the way here and not spend any time with her.

Since I'd canceled her trip, we'd only video-chatted once.

Suddenly, she was too goddamn busy.

I shook my head and got up from my desk, moving over to the closet that was in the back of my office. I took one of the suit jackets off the hanger and slipped an arm through each hole. I straightened my tie before I went into my private restroom.

It had been a stressful fucking day.

My beard was a mess. Most of the gel had worn out of my hair.

I dampened my hands under the faucet and rubbed them over my face, combing my whiskers before I worked them over my head, and then I came out of the restroom and saw Brett standing in my office.

"What are you doing for dinner tonight?" he asked, leaning on the edge of my desk. "You want to grab something to eat with James and me?"

I went over to the other side of it, grabbed my phone, and tucked it into the inside pocket of my jacket. "I'm meeting up with Kristin."

He turned around to face me. "Wait, you mean, Kristin Evans?"

I nodded. "Whom else would I be talking about?"

"Shit, I know we discussed her before, but I didn't think you two would actually meet up again."

"Why?"

"Dude, you know why."

"Jesus Christ," I groaned. "Don't start with me. It's fucking dinner. Nothing else." I took my keys out of my desk, and he followed me to the door. Just as I closed it behind us, I said, "We've got a meeting tomorrow morning with Scarlett. Do you know what it's about?"

"I've tried to get her to tell me, but she won't budge. It's been on our calendar for weeks, so something must be up." He stopped in the doorway when we reached his office. "I asked Jack, and he doesn't know anything either."

"I'm sure it's something to do with LA."

"I don't know, man. She's been texting us most of that info."

I shrugged. "I'll see you in the morning," I said.

Then, I walked down the rest of the hallway and cut out the back door. There, I took the service elevator to the garage where I slipped into the driver's seat of my car, and then I headed toward South Beach.

Kristin had picked the restaurant we were meeting at.

She was more of a foodie than me, so I'd wanted her to decide.

She'd chosen a good one; I'd been there many times.

One of those times was with Eve.

When I pulled up to the front of the restaurant, I handed the keys to the valet attendant, and I went inside to notify the hostess of the reservation.

Once I gave her my name, she looked up from her tablet and said, "The other member of your party is already here. Please follow me."

As she led me through the dining room and toward a window that overlooked Collins Avenue, my eyes locked with Kristin's. And hers didn't let go of me until I kissed her on the cheek.

"Always late."

I laughed and took the seat across from hers. "Always so goddamn punctual."

I could smell her scent in the air. It hadn't changed. All these years later, and it still reminded me of a fucking sugar cookie.

I didn't miss it.

And I hated those goddamn cookies.

Still, it felt good to be in this place with her. It was so much healthier than the fighting and yelling and tears that had been shed the night before I moved to Florida.

"Enjoying Miami?" I asked her.

"Very much so."

Before she could say another word, the waiter came up to our table, holding a bottle of cabernet sauvignon. It was a brand that I knew extremely well because it was one of my favorites.

Kristin had remembered.

"I was told the two of you would be sharing this bottle," the waiter said to me.

I nodded, and again, he held the wine in my direction to show me a close-up of the label.

I glanced at Kristin. "You don't forget any details, do you?"

"Not usually."

The wine was uncorked, and the waiter poured me a tasting. I swallowed, approved the bottle, and waited until he filled both glasses before I said, "How long are you in town for?"

I was sure she'd told me at some point.

But I hadn't listened.

"A lot longer than I originally planned." She lifted her glass and held it in the air for a cheers. "To the both of us living in Miami."

What the fuck did she just say?

"You're moving here?"

She clanked her glass against mine. "I am indeed."

Talk about fucking irony.

I couldn't get her to leave LA and move to Miami when we opened The Agency. Instead, she'd ended our engagement and stuck around California for several years before she went to Brazil. *Now, after being gone for three years, she suddenly wants to move to Florida?*

"What made you change your mind?" I asked.

She wrapped her small fingers around the stem of the glass, turning it so that the wine swished up the sides. "There are two things. First, I checked out all the restaurants in LA that wanted to hire me, and none of them were good enough." She took a sip, staring at the rim of her glass, her eyes gradually lifting to meet mine. "I don't want what everyone expects out of me. I want to do something different."

"LA is expected. Miami isn't."

"Exactly." Her thumb ran over the section of glass she'd been staring at. "I'm tired of being only an employee. This time, I want a stake in the business. I want to be proud of something besides just the menu."

"I can understand that."

"There's one other reason I'm moving here."

"And that is?"

She paused, dropping her hand from the glass and resting both of them over the table, which she used to lean her body against, moving even closer to me. "You."

SEVENTEEN
EVE

"HEY," James said as I answered her call, her voice sounding slightly manic. "What are you doing right now?"

Using my shoulder to hold the phone, I got the front door open and walked inside my house, flipping on the lights. "I just got home. Why?"

"Are you alone?"

I laughed. "What is that supposed to mean?"

"I just meant, do you have any friends over, or is it just you?"

I dropped my bag on the couch and went into the kitchen to pour myself a glass of wine. "I'm alone. What's up, girl? You sound a little nutty."

"I have something to tell you, and I don't want it to freak you out."

I opened the fridge and took out one of the bottles of white. "Well, that's one way to get my attention."

"God, I'm so sorry. I don't know how to do this."

"Do what, James? You're starting to worry me."

I poured the wine into a stemless glass and brought it into my bedroom where I kicked off my shoes and took a seat on my bed.

After a sip, I pushed my back against the headboard and stretched my legs over the mattress.

"I promised Brett I wasn't going to tell you this. I'm literally hiding in the guest bathroom right now, so he doesn't hear me on the phone with you."

My feet dropped off the bed. "What the fuck? Are you okay? Did something happen?"

"It has nothing to do with me. I'm fine."

Relief washed over me, and I was able to relax again. "Then, what is this about?"

"You."

Me?

"Please start talking, James, before I really do freak out."

I heard her take a deep breath, and then she started with, "Brett and I were out to dinner tonight. We went to this little place on South Beach that we've gone to before. Anyway, we're sitting at our table in the corner, and guess who walks in?"

"I don't know."

And I didn't.

This conversation could go in so many directions; I had no idea who I should be thinking of.

"Max." She took another breath. "Picture this, okay? Max walks into the restaurant, and Brett's back is to him. So, I tell Brett that Max is here, and we should invite him to eat with us. But, as Brett turns around to look at Max, he tells me that's not a good idea. I couldn't imagine why Brett would say that until I watched Max move across the dining room and sit at a table with some chick."

"Okay." It was the wrong word. I just didn't know what else to say, but I knew something had to come out, so she'd know I was still on the line.

"Wait, has Max called you to tell you this already?"

"No." I took a breath, and it stung. "I have no idea what you're talking about."

"Listen, the guys eat with women all the time—clients, associates, other agents. I think nothing of it, and I would never make a big deal about it. But I didn't like the way this chick was looking at Max or how she was smiling at him, and I didn't like the way she had the waiter take a picture of them. Something just felt really off."

I didn't like the feeling in my stomach.

I didn't like the way my hands wouldn't stop shaking. How I was no longer resting across the bed but pacing my bedroom.

"I didn't ask Brett who she was at the restaurant because I didn't want to make a big deal about it there," she continued. "But, during the drive home, I did some digging. Wouldn't you know that the bitch had posted the picture on social media, tagged Max, and put the caption, *Him*, with a heart next to it?"

My throat felt so tight. "James—"

"When I saw that post, I lost my damn mind. I showed Brett and asked him who the hell she was. Girl, I was not at all prepared for the answer he gave me."

I stopped at the foot of my bed.

It felt like my heart was pounding out of my chest. My stomach was queasy.

Nothing felt right, and I could tell by the sound of her voice that the story was only going to get worse.

"What did Brett say?" I asked her.

She sighed, the noise sounding as sick as I felt. "That the woman is Kristin Evans."

"Max's ex-fiancée," we both said at the same time.

I knew who she was.

Max and I had briefly spoken about her in the past. He'd told me they dated through college, and they'd mostly lived together up until he moved to Florida. That was when she had ended things between them.

I didn't know why.

I just assumed she hadn't loved him enough to go.

When I'd first learned about her, I'd looked her up on social media. I had seen that she was a chef and was working at a place in South America. But that had been a while ago, so maybe she had moved back.

Or she was visiting.

Or he had asked her to come.

My throat was getting even tighter, making it hard to breathe.

"I didn't know they were having dinner tonight," I said. "I didn't even know they'd been in contact."

Tonight would have been one of the evenings I spent with Max in Miami had he not canceled my trip. The only reason I had been able to make it work was because the team from Horse Feathers had some flexibility with the date they were arriving, so I'd tried to rearrange things to see him. I'd thought we needed the time together, especially since I'd left Punta Cana so upset. I just wanted to talk to him in person and explain why I was feeling this way.

But he hadn't given me the chance.

He'd called me the next morning and said the dates wouldn't work.

He was too busy.

And, now, I knew the reason was because of his ex.

I felt like I was going to be ill.

"You know, I was supposed to be with him tonight," I whispered.

"I know."

I dropped my ass onto the edge of the bed and gripped it with one of my hands, squeezing the blanket between my fingers. "Why didn't he tell me, James? Why did he say nothing about her? All he did was text me earlier and ask if we could video-chat later tonight. You would think he would have at least mentioned he was going to dinner with her."

"And, with everything he's said to you lately, and then you add in this..."

"Oh God."

There were tears. I wasn't sure where they had come from. If they were out of anger or sadness or fear. I just knew they were streaming down my face, and my body was shaking so hard.

"Eve, listen to me, I don't want you to call him tonight. You're upset, clearly. So, I want you to take a minute and think about this, and then talk to him after you've had some sleep."

She didn't want me to call him, screaming like a lunatic.

I got it.

Because, as much as I wanted to yell, it would only put him on the attack, and it would solve nothing.

But screaming would feel so good right now.

"I'll wait until tomorrow," I promised.

"Are you okay?"

I closed my eyes, feeling the wetness mash between my lashes. "No." I tried to settle the pounding inside my chest. "I'm angry and disappointed and sad and gutted, and I'm really fucking pissed."

"If you need me, you know to call me anytime. I'll answer the phone, no matter what time it is."

I was sure Brett had told James not to tell me and definitely not to get involved in this, so I imagined this was probably going to start a war between them. I was sure Max would say something to Brett about it, too.

But James didn't care.

She had my back.

She always did.

"Thank you," I said softly.

"Anything for you."

I hung up and stared at the blank screen of my phone, the emotions pouring out of me in waves.

Why?

I'd never questioned who he ate with or hung out with or went to the bars with. That was because I trusted him. Enough so that I'd brought other women into our bed. And I'd watched him fuck each one of them.

Never once had I gotten jealous.

It just wasn't a trait I possessed.

That was why I didn't understand his reasoning for keeping Kristin a secret.

Why he'd said he had business meetings both nights.

She certainly wasn't what I would consider work.

What made it even worse was that he had canceled on me to be with her.

God, he was such a dick.

I knew I should put my phone down and not pick it back up. I knew I definitely shouldn't click the social media app where Kristin had her account. But my hands were moving so fast, and I couldn't stop them.

Once the app was open, I clicked on the search bar and typed in her name.

Her profile came right up.

And the picture of her and Max was there.

The shot had been taken at their table. They were sitting on opposite sides and leaning in to get closer. He was smiling at the camera, but she was looking at him with a grin that covered her whole goddamn face.

Him with a heart.

"How could you do this to me?" I gritted between my teeth.

Just as I went to look away, a text came across the screen, and Max's name was at the top of the alert.

I took a deep breath, willing some of the sickness to go away, and I clicked on the text box.

Max: You free? Let's video-chat.

The phone fell from my hand, and I hurried into the bathroom, turning on the water to fill the tub. Once it was set to warm, I went to the fridge and grabbed the whole bottle of wine, bringing it back into the bathroom.

I ditched my clothes and slid in.

I could hear my phone beeping from the floor of my room, telling me more messages were coming in.

I didn't care what any of them said.

None of them could take this feeling away.

EIGHTEEN
MAX

BRETT, Jack, and I sat around the conference room table, drinking from our coffee mugs and waiting for Scarlett to walk in. We'd stopped by her office on our way here, and she'd told us she was running some numbers and would be down in a few seconds.

That was fifteen minutes ago.

I could tell the guys were getting as restless as me.

"What the fuck?" Jack said as he looked at the time on the wall clock. "This isn't like Scarlett at all. She's usually the first one in here."

"And Max is usually the last," Brett said.

"Yeah, yeah," I groaned. "Maybe she's putting out a fire. I know my department processed a shit-ton of contracts today. Something could have gone wrong."

"I don't think so," Brett responded. "I think she's still working on whatever she's presenting to us."

I shook my head. "Scarlett's more prepared than that. She's been planning this meeting for weeks. Whatever she has to show us, it's been well calculated and rehearsed."

"Who the fuck knows?" Jack said. "I just wish she'd hurry up.

As soon as this is over, Samantha and I are taking Lucy to Jacksonville to catch tonight's game, and then we're flying back tomorrow morning."

"She's becoming quite the little agent," Brett said.

"Are you kidding me? She's the best business partner I could ever have. Whenever she's around one of my athletes, they turn all fucking mushy, and they can't say no to her. I'm going to start bringing her to every negotiation." He nodded toward Brett. "You'll see what I mean very soon."

"What?" I chimed in. "James is fucking pregnant?"

"No, she's not pregnant," Jack answered. "At least, not that I've heard. But, knowing Brett, he'll knock her up within a few months of getting hitched, so he can keep her planted in Miami for a while."

Brett laughed. "That's not a bad idea, man. Getting James pregnant is the only way I'll ever slow her down."

What the fuck am I listening to?

The two of them looked at me just as Jack said, "When the hell are you going to ask Eve to marry you?"

"Oh, hell no. Go back to the kid talk or whatever it was that you two were discussing. You're not going to shine your flashlights on me now, motherfuckers."

Jack took a long drink from his coffee. "Jesus, you mention one thing about marriage, and he turns into the biggest—"

"Don't finish that thought," Scarlett said as she walked into the room. Holding several folders in her hands, she carried them to the head of the table where she took a seat. "I'm going to get right to it."

"We're good with that," Brett replied.

Jack and I nodded.

She rested her hands on top of the folders, her stare moving around to each of us. "I've been approached by a management company. They would like to work with us."

A business looking for referrals? That wasn't what I'd expected.

But that made this one of the easiest conversations we'd ever have.

"We already work with several," I said. "If this one is legit, we'll have one of the assistants check them out, and I'm sure we'll be able to add them to our master list of managers."

Her eyes settled on me. "We'd be getting rid of our master list, and we'd no longer be referring the business to managers elsewhere. We'd be keeping it in-house."

"You're saying, they want to become business partners?" Jack said.

She nodded. "That's right."

Partners?

Several companies had approached us in the past to do the same thing. It wasn't something we'd ever considered.

But none of the companies had been management firms either.

"Who are they?" Brett asked.

"Entertainment Management Worldwide."

My brows rose, as I was surprised by the name she'd just thrown out.

"I know of them," I said. "They work with several of my clients."

"They work with mine, too," Jack said.

"And mine," Brett agreed. "Why do they want to partner with us?"

This was where the selling came in, and she was up against the three hardest negotiators in the business.

Scarlett shifted in her chair and leaned back just a little, a grin spreading across her face the whole time. "We're the largest agency of our kind on the East Coast. After we expand to LA, within a few years, my forecasts show we'll be taking over the

West Coast as well. Our client list is tremendous, and we've expanded into PR, which brings in a whole new segment of clients who can and will be agented at some point. The question is, why wouldn't they want to work with us?"

"Of course, because they'd be walking into a sure thing," Jack said, twisting back and forth in his seat. "They know, if we suggest their management to our clients, most will eventually sign. The department would triple its revenue within the first day."

"On the flip side, do you know how many clients we'll earn for the agency side?" Scarlett asked. When no one answered, she added, "I think you're underestimating their reach and who's signed with them." She pulled out several sheets from the folders and handed one to each of us. "I believe you'll find a majority of your personal clients listed on that paper."

She was right.

Entertainment Management Worldwide was much larger than I'd thought.

"In a market like today's, our talent is stretched thinner than ever," Scarlett said. "Celebrities are looking for convenience. They want to take the least amount of time to accomplish things. Being able to offer other services makes us more desirable. It also makes it harder for a client to leave us because we'll have such a large stake of their business."

There was one question no one had asked yet.

And it was the most important.

I leaned my body into the table and said, "What do the numbers look like?"

She took out another stack of papers, which turned out to be multiple spreadsheets stapled together, and she handed them to us. Then, she pointed at the first page. "I've been going over their books for the first three quarters of last year. They just sent me the fourth quarter last night, which was what I was working on this morning. I've calculated every scenario, one that even includes losing thirty percent of their client base upon the merger."

"You know we wouldn't let that happen," Jack said.

"I know, but I need to look at every possibility to determine the risk." She flipped to page six and waited for us to catch up. "Even in that case, the result is in red at the bottom of the page."

"Jesus Christ," Brett sighed. "You're sure that's losing, not gaining thirty percent?"

She nodded again. "I'm positive."

These figures were impressive as fuck.

So, they didn't just have a client list that shocked the hell out of me. They had more profit than I ever would have guessed. No debt, no receivables, just one sexy-looking bottom line.

"I need to know more," I told her. "This looks too good to be true."

"They have two offices—LA and Manhattan," Scarlett said. "Two hundred managers in New York and one fifty in LA. There are three partners, all our age. They met in LA after college, worked PA jobs for a bunch of actors while they learned the business, and then they started with a small client load. Slowly, it grew from there."

"Their story isn't that far off from ours," Brett said.

"It's not," she agreed. She sat closer to the table, leaning over it as she glanced at the three of us. "They're hungry. They're fighters. They have the same drive that wakes each one of us up at five in the morning, forcing our asses to get to work and gain one more point of the market. They're us, I'm telling you."

Scarlett wasn't a bullshitter.

She also wasn't a salesperson.

She was all about numbers, and all she stated was facts.

Therefore, I believed everything she was saying.

I just didn't know if this move was right for us.

"Do you have a copy of the contract?" I asked.

She removed the last stack of papers and handed them around the table. The contract was over forty pages long. It would take some time to read through it and decide if, legally and financially, this was something worth pursuing.

"Just in case, I sent a copy to our in-house counsel this morning. He'll be reading it with you and available to answer any questions," she told us.

"I need some time," Jack said. "To study this, to think about it. I don't want to be rushed."

"You won't be." She pulled out her phone, tapped the screen a few times, and showed us her calendar. "I've already scheduled another time for all of us to get together again and chat about your thoughts." She pulled the folders into her arms and held them against her chest.

"Any other surprises?" Brett asked her.

"No." She smiled. "I'm done torturing you for today."

The four of us stood from the table and moved toward the door. We said nothing as we walked through it, and the silence wasn't broken until we reached Brett's office.

"Three more bosses?"

It was just the two of us. Jack had gone to his office, and Scarlett had gone to hers.

"I'm worried about that, too," I admitted. "But we could keep them in LA and Manhattan and leave Miami for us. And it would certainly solve the issue as to who'd be running LA."

"That's a good point." He looked down the hall toward the section of desks that were occupied by his team. "You think this is a good idea?"

I really considered his question before I said, "Scarlett knows her shit. She knows what we want out of this industry. If she didn't think we could dominate the management world, she never would have presented it to us."

He shook his head. "You know, this might bring us one step closer to the top."

I smiled. "Don't get too excited yet. This isn't going to be fucking cheap."

He patted my shoulder, and I continued moving down the hall until I reached my door. Once I was inside my office, I checked my phone.

Eve still hadn't replied to the goddamn text I sent her last night.

That wasn't like her.

Even if her answer was short, she always wrote something back.

I hit the screen and started typing.

Me: Good morning, baby.

NINETEEN
EVE

James: Have you spoken to Max?
Me: I have my meeting with Horse Feathers in a few minutes, so I haven't reached out to him yet.
James: OMG, I completely forgot that was today. You need to call me right after and tell me all the details.
Me: Okay.
James: Eve, you're going to be all right. Go kick ass. Love you.

I SAT in my car outside the restaurant, holding my phone in my hand, staring at James's texts.

You're going to be all right.

Last night, I wouldn't have agreed with that statement.

My emotions had turned so dark while I was in the tub, and they'd lasted up until four o'clock this morning when I passed out. It had been too much to process all at once and trying to had caused me to break down.

The first bottle of wine hadn't helped.

Neither had the second.

And, if this meeting with Horse Feathers hadn't been scheduled for lunchtime, I probably would have missed it from my hangover being so severe. But, since I'd had a few hours to rally, I'd had time to put some food in my stomach to settle it, drink some strong coffee, and down a mix of vitamins that were overdosing me with electrolytes.

Remembering the night I'd just experienced was the reason I didn't check the other messages that had come through my phone. I knew at least one was from Max. I wasn't ready for his words, especially not when I was still this raw.

So, instead of reading them, I tossed my phone in my bag, turned off the car, and walked inside the restaurant. I gave my name to the hostess, and she led me through the main dining room.

"I'm taking you to a private room in the back where you'll meet your other guests," she said over her shoulder.

I hadn't expected private.

I hadn't expected to feel this nervous either, but that energy was growing more with each step I took.

"Thank you," I responded, and I continued to follow her.

When we reached the back of the restaurant, she stopped just to the side of the only open door. "Go ahead in. I'll shut the door behind you to give you some privacy."

I nodded and kept moving, and the sound of my heels instantly caught the attention of the people in the room.

I took a quick glance at all three faces and locked eyes with the man who was standing to greet me.

"Miss Kennedy," he said, reaching for my hand. "I'm Alberto Romano."

I was startled by how attractive he was. His salt-and-pepper hair was slicked back, and he had eyes that were positively piercing and olive skin that was perfectly sun-kissed.

"It's nice to meet you," I said, feeling him gently squeeze my hand.

"It's an honor." He smiled, and the lines around his mouth and the ones to the sides of his eyes deepened. "Please let me introduce you to my team."

I broke eye contact to glance at the man and woman sitting at the table. They were at least ten years younger than Alberto, somewhere in their thirties, and they were just as attractive, both bearing grins that immediately caused me to return the gesture.

"This is Maria, our lead designer for women's apparel," Alberto said, and I shook her hand. "And this is Enzo, our lead designer for women's accessories."

My fingers then moved to Enzo's grip.

"Please sit," Alberto said, pointing to the chair closest to me.

I draped my bag over the corner of the wood and sat on the leather cushion.

"Miss Kennedy—"

"Eve, please," I interrupted and took a deep breath, hoping it would calm me.

"Eve," Alberto started again. "Thank you so much for meeting with us. We've really been looking forward to this."

"Me, too."

Curiosity had picked away at me during the last few days, and I still couldn't imagine what this whole thing was about.

"Like I said in my email," Alberto said, "Horse Feathers has now been in business for a little over three years. In that short period of time, we've had an incredible amount of success. Our clothes are now sold across the globe, and because of people like you, we've had some of the biggest-named celebrities wear our designs."

"We're blessed," Maria said as she put her hand over her heart.

Enzo nodded. "It's been a dream."

Alberto took a drink from his water and then said, "Our designs are influenced by mood. We feel our surroundings and translate them into emotions. Each piece is part of that mood, like a tiny branch that's weaved together into a collection or a nest." I heard the air exhaled through his nose as his fingers raked across his thick beard. "The practice has served us well, but it's not enough. We need more."

I still couldn't figure out how I fit into all of this, and nothing he'd said was giving me any clues. But it wasn't time to ask those questions yet because I could tell he wasn't done talking.

When his hand dropped onto the table, he smiled again and said, "Something is missing from our business—a factor that we hadn't taken into consideration until now. You see, our typical client doesn't walk into a store and purchase our clothing. Most transactions take place with a stylist or personal shopper. Then, you're the ones responsible for putting the outfit together. So, don't you see, Eve? You're the missing link."

I waited for a deeper explanation. When I didn't get one, I said, "I'm not sure I know what you mean."

"You know what a piece of clothing is going to look like on a body, you know how it should be presented to make it more appealing to a certain audience, you know what it should be paired with. And you know what our audience is looking for. That right there is a vision, and it's one we don't have. That's why we want you to be a part of designing our brand."

I blinked several times as I took in what he'd just said.

"I'm still not sure I understand," I said, using the softest voice I had.

"Miss Kenn—Eve, we want you to help design our summer collection, which will debut on the runways of New York, Paris, and Rome a year from now."

He wanted me to help design.

An entire line.

That would be walking down runways in top fashion markets of the world.

I die.

"Before you say anything," he continued, "let's go over the logistics, so you understand your role a little bit better."

"Okay."

I wanted to say so much more, but I couldn't.

I was too shocked.

Too consumed.

Too overwhelmed.

"The position would require you to move to Milan and live there for six months. We will provide housing and everything you'll need while you're there. At the end of your contract, you'll have a few different options; you can renew and stay in Italy, work remotely back in the States and fly in quarterly, or not work with us at all."

Alberto nodded toward Maria, and she cleared her throat and took over. "During the six months, you'll work with us in our design center. Because we understand what we're asking from you, we'll only require you to be in our office three hours a day, five days a week. You're free to do whatever you want during the rest of the time, such as continuing to work on your company, which we know is vital for running a business as successful as yours."

"Now, onto the pay," Alberto said.

He reached behind him into a briefcase that was on the floor, pulled out some papers, and set them in front of me. It was a contract. On the first page, just after my contact information, were the terms.

Six months in Milan.

One million dollars.

I stared at the number, waiting for it to change, expecting one of them to rip the sheet of paper out from under my hands and say the figure was a mistake and that they'd offered way too much. Because they certainly couldn't think my time was worth one million dollars.

I slowly looked up at Alberto, knowing I would never catch my breath again.

"We know this is something you need to think about," Alberto said. "We don't expect you to make a decision right now, but we're hoping you'll give us one within a week."

A week?

So, within the next seven days, I had to come up with an answer to a question I still couldn't wrap my head around.

"I can do that," I said, hoping it wasn't a lie.

"If you agree to sign on, we'll be looking for you to start in two to three weeks," Enzo said. "We'll give you a few days to get settled in your apartment, and then we'll get to work."

My own apartment.

In Milan.

This wasn't really happening.

It couldn't be.

"I would just like to remind you of something," Alberto said. "We don't expect you to pause the business you've created here or to lose everything you've worked so hard for. That's why the position offers plenty of flexibility, so you can spend a short amount of time with us and the rest of the day doing what you need for your clients."

An assistant can pull from the showrooms based on pictures sent to me the day before. Outfits photographed and approved through email. A second assistant to help with fittings.

My brain was going so fast.

It was solving problems that would arise while I wasn't here.

It needed to stop and breathe for a second.

And I needed to say something.

I tried to fill my lungs with air while I scanned each of their faces, all of them so encouraging, all of them wanting me to say yes.

"It's the offer of a lifetime," I admitted. "And it's something I never thought would ever come my way, and I'm still completely speechless over it."

"It's a lot to consider, Eve."

"It is," I said, agreeing with Maria. "I promise I'll weigh your suggestions, and I'll come up with an answer within a week."

"Wonderful," Alberto said.

"I'm very pleased to hear that," Maria replied.

"Now, won't you please stay for lunch?" Enzo asked. "We hear this restaurant is quite tasty."

I wanted nothing more than to run to my car and scream as loud as I could and call James so that I could freak out with someone over this.

But that wouldn't be smart.

I needed to stay and get a better feel for the people I could potentially be working with.

So, I grinned and nodded and said, "Yes. I would love to."

TWENTY
EVE

James: Did I dream the conversation we had earlier today, or did it really happen? Because, if it really happened, that means my best friend really got asked to codesign a designer's summer collection.

Me: Pinch me, girl. Please. This is my second bath of the day, and besides being really fucking clean, I'm waiting to just melt into the water.

James: Have you made a decision already, or are you still screaming?

Me: No decision. It's too soon. But, every few minutes, I scream. Just because.

James: You deserve it.

Me: I have so much adulting to do right now.

James: I wouldn't want to be you.

Me: I know. Plus, I still haven't returned his text. So, there's that...

James: At least give him a one-worded response by tonight. If not, I'm sure he's going to get worried and then he'll track me down through Brett and I'll have to tell him he's a fucking asshole for going out to dinner with that bitch last night. You don't want me to do that.

Me: I'll respond to him.

James: Are you going to tell him about Italy at the same time?

Me: I don't know, but I know it's a conversation we'll have to have over the phone because he's not planning on seeing me for another few weeks, and I'm going to have to make a decision before that.

James: Good God.

Me: I'll call you in the morning.

James: You'd better.

TWENTY-ONE
MAX

THE RINGING of my phone woke me up.

I glanced toward my nightstand and saw that my cell wasn't there, so I sat up and looked for it on the bed. The movement was what caused me to feel it. I was clenching it against my palm, fingers squeezing the hard plastic cover.

I didn't remember passing out.

I only remembered checking the time on my phone, and that had been over two hours ago. At that point, I still hadn't heard from Eve.

Now, her name was lighting up my goddamn screen.

"Where the fuck have you been?" I said as I answered.

She said nothing, but I heard her breathing, and it was loud enough to know she was there.

Seconds passed.

And then, "I needed some time."

I kicked off the sheet and blanket, rubbing my hand over my bare abs. "For what?"

"To think."

It didn't even sound like her.

Her voice was flat, like all the emotion and excitement had been drained from it.

"What's going on with you?"

She sighed, and that was when something finally came through.

Pain.

"How much do you care about me, Max?"

How much do I care about her?

What kind of bullshit is that?

The Eve I knew would never need to ask that kind of question.

"You know how much."

I heard her breathe several more times.

"Enough to give me more?"

"More of what?" I reached for the remote and turned off the TV, which I must have forgotten to do before I'd fallen asleep. "What's gotten into you?"

"I know you're comfortable with the way things are between us, and I know it's worked for a long time. But I need more from you. And, every time I drop a hint, trying to tell you what I want, you respond in a way that disappoints me."

"Like what?"

I heard her laugh, but I knew she didn't find this funny.

"When I told you that you should come run the LA office, you said nothing in this world could make you move back to California."

"What's wrong with what I said?"

"Everything is wrong with it." I could tell she was fighting back tears. "I want you to move to LA, so I can spend more time with you. But I'm not even enough for you to consider it."

I didn't understand where this was coming from.

I'd never said that.

Eve was good.

She was better than fucking good.

"That answer had nothing to do with you," I said.

"That's the problem, Max. I wish it had. I wish all your answers had more to do with me."

Sure, she'd been a little different lately. Tenser. Even a little less sexual than normal. But I'd just assumed she was distracted with work.

I never thought it had anything to do with our relationship.

"Eve, what do you want from me?"

She didn't respond right away. "I want more."

"How? I've already given you everything."

When she exhaled, the pain in her breath was even more distinct. "I know you don't mean that. You couldn't possibly. Because, if you think that's everything, then I'm terrified to know what you think is nothing."

"Eve—"

"Max, I see you only every few weeks, and now, it's down to once a month. And, most of the time we're together, you're working and always on your phone. I get late-night calls when you're minutes away from falling asleep. I get the code that lets me inside your house. That's it."

That was more than any girl had gotten since Kristin.

And, now, it wasn't enough.

"I thought you loved what we had."

"God, I wish you'd do less thinking." Her voice was turning sharp. "Every time you do, you come up with an idea of what you think I want, and it couldn't be further from the truth."

"Now, I really don't know what you're talking about."

"A family, Max. Why would you ever assume that I don't want one?"

I swung my legs over the bed and dropped my feet onto the floor, and then I walked over to the wall of windows. The glass was freezing against my bare skin.

I fucking needed the cold right now.

It was the only thing keeping me calm.

"I've been with you for two years," I said. "Never once have you brought up having children. Therefore, I assumed you didn't want any. Unless you tell me otherwise, how am I supposed to know, Eve?"

"This isn't my fault."

I shook my head, tugging at the ends of my hair. "No one is blaming you."

"I want more."

There was that goddamn word again.

"What's more?"

"Move to LA and take over that office."

My eyes flicked through the glass to the backyard where the moon was lighting up Biscayne Bay. "No."

"Then, what you're saying is, if I want to take our relationship to the next level and spend more time with you, I have to give up my clients? My business? Everything I've built here?"

My other hand moved to the window, and I pressed my palm against it. "I didn't say that."

Silence ticked between us, and then her voice got extremely quiet as she said, "I was offered a job today that would require me to move to Italy for six months. I'd be working with a designer to create their summer collection."

"Sounds like something you'd want to do."

"But what I want is you, Max. I want to wake up next to you every morning. I want to eat breakfast with you when we get home from the gym. I want to jump in the shower with you as you're getting ready for work. I want to see your face over candlelight. I want your lips to be the last thing I kiss before I close my eyes." She took a few more breaths, and I heard so much emotion coming out of her. "Tell me not to go. Tell me not to take the job in Italy. Tell me you'll figure out a way to give me more."

I pounded my fist against the window, hitting it until the skin turned raw.

There was so much need in her voice.

So much sadness in each sob.

One word would take it all away.

But I couldn't fucking say it.

I wouldn't do that to her.

I wasn't the kind of guy who would ever tell her to give up her dreams.

Because I had ones of my own that I still needed to accomplish, and I would never want her to take those away from me.

"I won't do that," I told her.

"Then, tell me you'll meet me in the middle, so I won't be the only one sacrificing. Tell me you'll consider LA."

I pressed my forehead against the glass. "Eve..."

"Tell me you'll come to California to be with me."

My eyes closed.

My heart fucking pounded against my chest.

I released a long, deep breath. "I won't do that either."

"Then, I know what I have to do."

I didn't hear another thing because she disconnected the call.

TWENTY-TWO
MAX

Me: It's been fucking days since I've heard your voice. Why won't you call me back?
Eve: I've been busy.
Me: I need to talk to you.
Eve: I'll call you tonight.
Me: I'll be flying, so I'll call you. Answer your phone this time.

AS I SAT on the couch on the plane, I stared at the messages Eve and I had exchanged earlier today. Texting was the only way we'd been communicating, the only way she'd fucking talk to me since she phoned me in the middle of the night to tell me she wanted more.

That was four days ago.

And, every day, her texts had become a little more distant.

The conversation we'd had that night still didn't make any sense. I didn't understand when she'd suddenly become so unhappy. I'd never felt the change. I'd never known she resented my comments or that she was hinting at wanting more out of our relationship.

I wasn't a fucking mind reader. I wasn't the kind of guy who picked up breadcrumbs.

If she wanted something, she should have told me.

Because, for the last two years, I'd thought things were good between us. I'd thought we had the most unbelievable time whenever we were together. We never fought. There wasn't any jealousy. Our chemistry was off the fucking charts.

But she obviously didn't think things were as perfect as I did.

She wanted more of everything—more time together, more attention, a goddamn family, things I just couldn't give her right now. And the one thing I could possibly bend on, which was us living in the same city, I couldn't give her either because there was no way in hell I would move to LA. I hated everything about that place. I'd left it for a reason, and there was no way I was going back.

She had to understand that.

But, shit, I had a feeling she didn't understand anything at this moment.

Just as I shook my head, trying to clear out some of those thoughts, the sound of a zipper caught my attention. My eyes dragged to the other side of the plane where Brett was sitting.

He'd opened his computer bag, and he was putting his laptop inside it. Once he got it in there, he put his feet on the chair in front of him, grabbed his scotch, and turned toward me. "What the hell is going on?"

"You want to be a little more specific?"

He took a drink, keeping his stare on me. "James told me that Eve got a job offer in Italy."

I nodded.

"What are you going to do about it?"

I pointed at my chest. "What am I going to do about it? Nothing. The decision is on her, not me."

"You could tell her not to go."

"You know I won't do that. A move that big will change her whole career. I have no right to chime in on something like that." I crossed my foot over my knee and extended my arms over the top of the couch, gripping my scotch in my hand. "If James got an opportunity that would take her away, you'd do the same fucking thing. Because we're business people, and that's what we do."

He seemed to ponder that thought for several seconds before he responded, "I wouldn't fucking like it, but if it would take her career to the next level, then you're right."

"I know I'm fucking right, and I'm not saying I like it either." I took a drink, letting the burn settle over my tongue before I swallowed. "You want to know something? When I found out Kristin didn't want to go to Miami, I almost stayed in LA with her. I was just going to tell you guys I couldn't leave her, and my plan was to do everything I could to win her back."

"What made you change your mind?"

"The thought of not becoming the highest-earning music agent in the country. No way in hell was I going to let myself stay in second place, and that's right where I'd be if I didn't get away from our old company and start The Agency with you guys. Plus, I'd have so much regret if I watched you fuckers build the business of my dreams, and I wasn't a part of it."

"We would have handcuffed your ass and put you on a goddamn plane if you had told us you were staying in Cali."

"I figured that, too."

He leaned forward in his seat, his elbows now resting on his knees. "You've got to handle shit with her."

"I know."

I looked at my phone, pulling up the calendar to check the schedule my assistant had put together. "I'm on the road for the next four days, but I'll be seeing her at the end of the week. We'll get things figured out then."

"Good."

I took a few more sips of my scotch, and then I said, "I'm going to give her a call."

He pointed toward the back of the plane. "Go take the bedroom. I've got some work I need to finish up here."

I grabbed the satellite phone that we kept near the cockpit and went to the back of the plane, shutting the bedroom door behind me. The room was small as hell. A bed, TV, and a tiny table that was built into the wall were all that was in here. But it was perfect to nap in and even better to fuck in.

And Eve's bare ass had touched almost every surface in here.

Damn it.

I climbed onto the bed and dialed her number.

She answered after the second ring, "Eve Kennedy."

Her voice sounded nothing like the last time we had spoken. It was alive, full of energy, and there wasn't a tear anywhere near that gorgeous face.

God, I'd missed that tone.

Because the satellite phone showed up as *Unknown* on caller ID, I said, "It's me."

"Max, I don't have that long to talk. I'm heading to a fitting right now, and I have a conference call in about three minutes that I have to take in the car."

And then the sound that I loved so goddamn much was gone.

In its place was a voice that couldn't fucking be bothered.

Where the hell was the girl who would have told me how much she wanted me instead of how busy she was?

I needed that girl back.

"Hi," I said.

She took a breath. "Hey."

"Why has it taken so long to get you on the phone?"

"There were some things I needed to think about, and I couldn't do that if I was talking to you every day."

"Eve, you live on the other side of the country. How much space do you need?"

"You don't need to remind me. I know how far away you live." She sighed, and I could feel the tension in her body. "Where are you flying to?"

"Nashville. Talia is going to start recording, and I'm going to be there for the first few sessions. Then, I'll be swinging by Vegas for a photo shoot and then a show at Red Rocks. Finally, I'll be in LA for The Agency's soft opening."

"And to see me."

"Yes, and to see you. I think we need to talk."

"We do." I heard movement in the background—the sound of a car door closing and a quick blast of music before it was turned down. "My conference call is going to start any second. I have to go. I'll see you in a few days."

I closed my eyes.

There was nothing I could say to make this better. I just had to wait until I saw her in LA.

But I had to say something, goddamn it.

I raked my hand through my hair as I opened my eyes. "I've missed you like hell."

"Good-bye, Max."

And then the phone went dead.

TWENTY-THREE
EVE

WHILE LORRIE FINISHED PUTTING on my makeup and curling the ends of my hair, I stared at myself in the bathroom mirror. She'd used a light gloss on my lips and darkened my eyes with a smoky shadow, keeping the rest of my face in neutral tones. My hair was down, hanging in loose waves that accented my shoulders, which were open in the strapless dress.

And the dress couldn't have been more perfect.

It was tight. Seductive.

Extremely sensual.

It had been a month since our trip to Punta Cana, and I wanted Max to see me at my best.

Tonight, I certainly looked it.

"I think we're about done here," Lorrie said, pulling the glossy wand off my mouth where she'd just finished adding another layer. "Max is going to devour you when he sees you."

She would know.

She also knew what it felt like to be devoured by him.

The scene from that evening flashed in my head. God, that had been such a hot night.

But, since our threesome, it felt like so much had changed between Max and me.

The thought of that killed me.

And the place that we were in hurt me even more.

I stood from the chair and turned around to face her. "Thank you for making me beautiful."

She gave me a hug, squeezing for a second longer than she needed to. "When will I see you again?"

I shrugged as she released me, not knowing that answer. "Text me?"

"You can count on it," she said with a smile before she packed up her things.

She followed me out of the house where she got into her car, and I climbed into the back of the SUV that Max had sent.

Due to his schedule being so tight, he was going straight from the plane to the party. Since James was on location, filming in Boston, I would be riding solo. And, although I was close to Scarlett and the guys, they would be busy entertaining, so I knew I'd mostly be on my own tonight. I wouldn't even have Samantha to keep me company because Lucy had a dance recital that neither of her parents wanted her to miss.

Once I was settled in the backseat, the driver moved onto the road and headed for downtown. To keep my brain busy and off the conversation I knew I was going to have with Max, I spent the drive replying to emails and responding to the texts Trevor had sent. He was my new assistant. Someone I had stolen from Prada where he'd worked their showroom for the last two years. Since I pulled from that designer so often, I'd met Trevor when he first started working there. When I had seen his résumé come through my email, I'd immediately set up an interview and hired him on the spot.

The two of us had been logging sixteen-hour days to get him trained and introduced to all my clients and to establish a process that would work for us both. Within another week, he'd be able to do it all on his own.

I glanced up from my phone and saw that we were almost at the building, so I slipped my cell into my clutch, and I took several deep breaths. Then, I checked the top of my dress to make sure it was holding me in, and I tugged the bottom hem lower, so I wouldn't have to do it when I got out of the car.

When we came to a stop, the driver opened my door and gave me his hand to help me out. My heels hit the ground, and I quickly scanned the entrance. Since it was just the soft opening, there wasn't a red carpet. There also weren't any paparazzi camped outside.

I was so relieved.

It didn't matter how good I looked on the outside; my insides were churning. My smile was fake. Anxiety had to be showing in my eyes, so the last thing I wanted was for this feeling to be documented and shared publicly.

"I'll escort you up to the door," the driver said.

"No need." I released his hand. "But thank you."

He pointed to the side of the building. "I'll be parked right over there."

I nodded and made my way over to the security guard, who was standing in the doorway.

"Eve Kennedy," I said to him. "I'm a guest of Max Graham's."

His eyes moved to the tablet that he held in his hand. After a second, he said to the tuxedo-clad gentleman behind him, "Please escort Miss Kennedy to the elevator."

The man wearing the tux extended his arm, which I looped my hand through, and he brought me to the elevator inside the lobby. He didn't come into the elevator with me. He just reached over to the control panel and pressed a button. "Have a wonderful evening."

As the door closed, I pressed my back against the wall and

gripped the silver safety bar that ran across the middle. My hands were shaking. My body was tense. The heels, which normally were comfortable, were pinching my toes. I tried so hard to control my breathing, but it was getting more difficult with each floor I passed.

All of these emotions were over seeing Max, and the moment was almost here.

When the door slid open, the waiter standing just outside said, "Welcome to The Agency LA, Miss Kennedy."

I moved out of the elevator and took the champagne he'd handed to me, immediately bringing it up to my lips and swallowing almost half of it.

"I'm happy to give you a tour of the office—"

"I'm just going to walk around on my own," I said, and I went toward the reception area.

"No problem." He'd taken a few steps toward me, but he was now going back to the elevator. "Please let us know if you need anything."

Since I already knew the layout and I assumed where most of the attendees were hanging out, I turned in the opposite direction of where they were, and I headed for the executive offices.

I just needed a second alone before I spoke to him.

A second to catch my breath.

A second to get my thoughts straight because, now that I was in his space, I felt different than when I had been in the car.

I felt more shaken, more confused.

I wasn't sure I had ever been this raw before.

I stopped in the hallway across from the wall of windows, and I moved over to one of them. As I stood in front of it, I glanced at downtown LA, my free hand gripping the metal frame of the glass.

So many of my beginnings had happened in this town.

The first time I'd styled a client. The first showroom I'd ever been in. The first meeting I'd had with a designer. My first red-carpet premiere and awards show.

It was also where I'd been offered the opportunity of a lifetime.

"There you are," I heard from behind me.

Max.

That voice, despite the feelings that were flowing through me, always caused such an impact. My heart raced even faster, and my limbs felt weak.

Before I had a chance to respond, he was pressing his body against my back, his face dipping into the side of my neck, his hands clamping my waist.

He was too close.

Yet he wasn't close enough.

"God, I fucking missed you," he breathed in my ear.

For just a second, I closed my eyes.

I let his words simmer inside me, combined with the way he was touching me and the heat that was radiating off his body.

"You look gorgeous in this dress."

My eyes flicked open. "You haven't even seen all of me."

"I don't need to. The back is enough."

His voice deepened, almost sounding like a growl, and it caused me to turn around. Now that I was facing him, he leaned into the front of me, his face on the inside of my neck.

"Security told me you'd arrived. I'm surprised to find you back here."

"I wanted to check out the offices," I lied.

His lips touched my collarbone, and he kissed all around it. "I would have given you a tour."

His mouth felt so good. Too good.

But I needed it off me.

I took a step, so my back was now pushed against the cold

glass. He kept his hands on my waist, but at least his lips weren't touching me.

"I've been here before," I reminded him. "I don't need another tour."

His fingers lifted, traveling up my sides, and stopped when they reached my cheeks. Just when it looked like his mouth was about to dive toward me again, he said, "I know we need to talk. But, first, I want to taste you."

My breath hitched in my throat. "That isn't going to happen, Max."

His expression changed, the wrinkles between his brows deepening, his eyes squinting.

Things had been weird between us since I called him in the middle of the night and told him I wanted more. He couldn't possibly think we were just going to go back to the way things had been.

But, at the same time, he probably didn't know what to expect because we'd never really fought. We hardly ever disagreed. We were both always so happy to spend time together during our short visits that we soaked up every second before we went back to missing each other.

That was the pattern of long-distance relationships.

A pattern I just couldn't put up with anymore.

I tried to fill my lungs, squeezing in the air while trying to push out the words. "I've accepted the job in Italy." But, once those words came out, I regretted them. That wasn't what I'd planned on saying or how I wanted to start this conversation.

"Congratulations, baby. I think that's amazing."

"You...*do*?"

He nodded. "You can't turn down an opportunity like that."

The largest wave of emotion came over me, and I felt my body start to quiver. "No. No, no, no." I sucked in some air, feeling it burn all the way down to the bottom of my navel. "That's not what you were supposed to say."

"What are you talking about?"

My hands trembled at my sides, and I clutched them together and held them against my stomach to give me the courage to tell him how I felt. "When I pictured this moment..." I shook my head as the image came into my mind. It was so clear; I wanted to close my eyes and live in the dream instead of the reality I was facing here. "I pictured you gripping the tops of my arms as hard as you could and putting your face so close to mine and telling me not to go." The expression I saw in my head was nothing like the one he was giving me now. It was desperate, demanding, loving. But here, it was half-blank and half-bewildered. "I thought you'd tell me that you'd give me everything I wanted. That *more* would be possible because you were going to move to LA to be with me."

"I won't do that."

"But why?" My voice cracked. "Why won't you tell me not to go?"

"We've talked about this, Eve."

"Then, tell me again."

"I have dreams, too, you know. Things I want professionally that I haven't achieved. I would never want you to ask me to give those up, the same way I'd never ask you to do that for me."

I opened my mouth, and my chest shuddered. "Max, I just want you to love me."

"Eve—"

"I want you to fight for me. I want you to hold me in your arms and tell me that leaving will be the biggest mistake of my life."

I wanted *more.*

Where the hell is more?

Why isn't he giving it to me?

"I won't do that."

It felt like he had just slapped me in the face.

It felt like all the blood had been drained from my body.

And, when I went to speak, a knot so large lodged into the back of my throat. "I'll be gone for six months. I won't be returning to the States at all during that time."

"I'll try to come and visit, if my schedule allows it."

He'll try?

I didn't think I could feel worse.

But I was wrong.

"I can't believe that's all you're going to say to me."

He continued to stare into my eyes, his gaze intensifying, his lips finally parting. "What do you want from me?"

The pain in the back of my throat was unbearable. It was spreading into my chest and running to my fingers as I drove them into my stomach. "I think..." *Oh God.* The thought of where this was going, of what I had to do, of the words I needed to say—it all stabbed me as rough and as deep as his rejection. "I thought I could continue being happy with the way things were, but it's just not enough. I can't do this anymore. I need more, and unless you're willing to give it to me, then..."

"What will make you happy?"

More flashed through my mind—all the time we'd spend together, the closet that we'd share, the faces that were a perfect mix of us both. But, when I blinked, it was all gone, and in its place was the loneliness that I'd been feeling since I last saw him.

"I want the next step of our relationship. I want you to move to LA and live with me. I want the commitment, the kids. I want more time, more attention." I took a breath. "Love, Max. I want love."

"And what if I don't give you those things?"

"Then, we're done."

The muscles flexed in his jaw. His stare sharpened.

But the strongest reaction he had was his hands.

They dropped from my face, as though my skin had burned him.

"You're sure about that?" he asked.

No.

"Yes."

"You're fucking positive?"

Tears began to sting my eyes. "I just don't see any other option." I closed my lids, hard, wishing the tears away because I couldn't let him see those drips.

I couldn't turn weak.

But I couldn't tolerate the pain anymore either.

"Are you telling me, this is it?"

Air was no longer moving in and out of my lungs. It was stuck in my throat, and that was tightening to a pinhole.

"Yes."

His arm lifted above my head, his hand landing on the glass behind me. He was caging me in, and I couldn't move.

"I don't believe that's what you want."

My heart shattered.

My stomach rolled.

"I don't know how to make it any clearer. If you don't want more then I don't want to be with you anymore, Max."

"I tried so fucking hard." His voice had turned soft, a sound I'd never heard from him before.

"You didn't try hard enough."

He sighed, shaking his head, his arm leaving the window and sliding into his pocket. "This is bullshit."

My insides were screaming.

My body felt like it was going to crumble at any second and fall into a heap on the floor.

"I feel the same way," I whispered.

If I said another word, the tears would fall, and they wouldn't stop. Then, he'd be able to see right through my pain, and he'd know I didn't want the things I was saying, but I didn't know how else to make this work.

I'm just not enough for him.

Or I'm just not the woman he wants to have everything with.

God, that thought hurt so fucking much.

I couldn't stay here for another second. I couldn't keep looking at that face I loved so much, at those lips I dreamed about. At our future that was as ugly as the champagne glass I had just dropped and was now shattered all over the ground.

I stepped to the side, and just as I was parallel to him, he grabbed my wrist and turned me until his lips slammed against mine. With his other hand, he cupped my face, keeping me close, deepening the kiss with every second that passed.

It felt so good.

Better than anything that had ever touched me.

And I would miss it.

But, if I stayed here any longer, I'd be tossed over his shoulder and carried into one of the offices, and then I'd be naked within minutes.

That would contradict everything I'd just said to him.

That would be a beginning when tonight had to be the end.

So, I pulled my mouth away and slipped a few steps past him as I said, "Good-bye, Max."

I walked down the hallway.

I didn't look over my shoulder.

I couldn't.

I just had to get away and not see him again, so I continued hurrying toward the elevator. When I reached it, I told the waiter who was standing there that I needed to go to the lobby.

"Just a few seconds," he said. "It's on its way up right now."

I glanced behind me to make sure he hadn't followed me.

There were several people standing in the reception area, but none of them were him.

I didn't know if I was relieved or if that upset me even more.

By the time I turned back around, the door was opening, and a few guests were walking out.

One of them was Scarlett.

Our eyes connected, and she said, "Eve, hi. I'm so happy to see you."

The tears were on the verge of dripping, and if I stopped to talk to her, all I would do was cry. I didn't want her to see me like that, and I didn't want to hear her ask why I was upset.

So, I waved at her and rushed inside the empty elevator and pounded my finger against the L button.

"Eve—" Her voice was cut off as the door closed.

Once it started to move, I wrapped my arms around my stomach and squeezed, hoping the pressure would stop the churning inside my body. With my breath still lost, I tried to wheeze in some air in an attempt to fill my lungs. And, because my mind was spinning, I rested my head against the cold metal wall and tried to get my thoughts to slow.

It was too much.

All of it.

I just have to make it to the SUV, I told myself.

There, I could fall apart. There, I could shed my tears. There, I could let the last several minutes eat away at me.

There, I could process that my relationship with Max was over.

The door opened into the lobby, and I rushed through security and went out the front. I turned when I reached the side of the building. There were several SUVs parked along the curb, and I walked up to each one, looking through the window to see if my driver was behind the wheel. By the fourth car, I saw him, and I knocked on the glass.

When I heard the door unlock, I opened it and climbed into the backseat. "Please take me home. The same place where you picked me up."

He was watching me through the rearview mirror. "Is there anything I can get you? I think I have some tissues up here," he spoke in such a soft, calming voice.

I was sure that was because he'd heard the panic in mine, that he saw the tears streaming down my cheeks, that he saw the way my body was rocking back and forth over the seat.

I shook my head. "I don't need a tissue. I just need to get home."

"I understand."

As we began to move, I untucked my clutch from under my arm, not even remembering that I'd put it there. Once it was unzipped, I took out my phone and clicked on the email app. I opened my drafts and stared at the email that was in there.

Dear Alberto,
I would like to thank you and your team once again for coming all the way to Los Angeles to meet with me. It was a wonderful opportunity to hear about the inner workings of your company and how devoted and passionate you and your colleagues are about Horse Feathers.

From the moment I first walked into your LA showroom, I knew it was a brand that I had to keep my eye on. You've evolved with each collection. Your moods have strengthened. Now, as I look back at your past designs, I can see the tears in the fabric. The smiles. The joy. The sorrow.

I've thought long and hard about your offer, and given the flexibility that you're allowing me to have, I would like to accept. The signed contract is attached along with all the other financial and NDA documents you asked for.

In regard to the amount of time I'll need before I report to Milan, I would like to take the full three weeks that we discussed at lunch. It's going to take me that long to get my business in a place where I can physically leave it for six months. I hope that won't be a problem. Please let me know if it is.

Looking forward to the future,
Eve

I'd written it the night I told Max I wanted more.

I just hadn't sent it.

I didn't want to.

Because, in my mind, Max was going to give me everything I wanted. And, as much as I wanted to take the opportunity in Italy, I wanted my relationship with him more.

Now, *more* wasn't possible.

My finger hovered over the Send button, and my eyes closed.

My chest turned even tighter.

I can do this.

I can leave.

It would be the best thing for me now. I'd learn so much, I'd be able to help another company, and I'd expand into an international market.

I'd be able to run away from everything that reminded me of him.

When my eyes opened again, my finger dropped onto the screen, and I watched the email go through.

It was done.

We were done.

And, now, the job was mine.

TWENTY-FOUR
MAX

"MAX?" Scarlett said.

My eyes were focused on the conference room table that was in our new LA office. I was staring at the fucking wood, hoping this meeting would be over soon so that I could get back to the condo and polish off the bottle of scotch that I'd opened for breakfast.

"Yeah?" I barked.

"What's your opinion on all of this?" she asked.

I looked up, catching her eyes. "All of what?"

"The partnership. That's why we're here and what this meeting is about."

At this moment, merging with Entertainment Management Worldwide was the last fucking thing on my mind. But Scarlett had gathered the four of us here, so she could either get shit rolling or squash the whole idea.

I hadn't even had a chance to look at the goddamn contract. I'd told our in-house counsel to read it for me and give me the highlights, which he'd emailed to me yesterday morning, and I'd read it during my flight to LA.

"I'm good with whatever you all decide."

Her eyes widened. "I know you didn't just say that to me."

I swiveled in my chair to face the head of the table where she was sitting. "You've got a problem with what I just said?"

She leaned her stomach into the edge of the wood and clasped her hands together. "Yes, I have a fucking problem with it. This is our future, Max. This is all four of us giving up a piece of what we've worked so hard to achieve. This doesn't just mean expansion. It means change. More partners. More services. The merger of two LA offices and an additional office in New York City." Her eyes narrowed. "So, I need you to put aside whatever is bothering you, get your shit together, and make a decision without relying on Brett and Jack to do all the work for you."

I ground my teeth together and leaned back in my seat, swinging the chair from side to side.

Damn it, she was right.

This was important, and business always came first.

But, hell, I just didn't have it in me today.

While I tried to get my mind in a good place, Scarlett said, "Why don't you tell us what's going on?"

Brett looked at me and nodded, which was his way of urging me to open up. He knew what had gone down because Eve had called James last night after she got home from the soft opening, and she'd told James everything. James had then told Brett, and he'd called me this morning before the meeting to make sure I was all right. That was when I'd found out that he knew.

Scarlett had to know something was up between Eve and me. She'd come up to me at some point during the party and said she'd tried to talk to Eve. Eve had ignored her and taken off in the elevator, and Scarlett had wanted to know why. I'd told her I didn't know, and then I'd continued to drown myself in scotch.

The soft opening hadn't been the time or place to talk about my relationship.

Right now wasn't much better, but at least there weren't any clients around.

"Eve and I broke up."

"What?" Scarlett gasped, her mouth opening to show me she was really as shocked as she sounded. "I had an inkling that something was wrong based on the way she acted last night, but I'm floored to hear this news."

"Me, too, buddy," Jack said. "I thought things were real good between you two."

"So did I," I told them.

"Then, how did this happen?" Scarlett asked.

I pressed the back of my head against the cushion of the chair and closed my eyes, exhaling a long-drawn-out sigh. "She got a job offer in Italy and took it. She wanted me to stop her from going and tell her I'd move to LA to manage this office, so I'd be closer to her and give her the *more* that she kept asking for."

"What the hell is *more*?" Jack asked.

My eyes flicked open. "For us to move in together and live happily ever after with kids and all that kind of shit."

"If that's what she wants, why not give it to her?" Scarlett asked.

I dropped my elbows on the table, let my head fall against my hands, and rubbed them over my hair. "I did that once, and you all know how it turned out."

"Eve isn't Kristin," Brett said.

I looked up. "In my mind, I can't differentiate the two."

"Man, you've got to get past that," Jack said.

"Get past it?" I barked. "Fuck, have you forgotten how bad things got when Kristin left me? I crawled inside a goddamn bottle of scotch, and I would have stayed there had you three not pulled me out."

"She hurt you—"

"She fucking cheated on me," I growled, not letting Scarlett finish what she was saying. "She fell in love with the fucker and left me."

As I thought back to that time in my life, I felt the pain again in the pit of my stomach.

Kristin wasn't just some girl I'd dated.

I had been with her all through high school and college. She was supposed to be the girl I married, whom I had a family with, until she woke up one morning and told me she'd been sleeping with someone else.

She was in love with someone else.

She wasn't moving to Florida with me, and she was ending our engagement.

She was leaving me to be with the fucker.

She was done.

"Like I said, Eve isn't Kristin," Brett repeated. "She's loyal, she's fucking crazy about you, and she's not going to treat you the way Kristin did."

I rubbed my hands against my temples, feeling the headache start to kick in. "Don't you remember the vow I made all those years ago? When I told you all that I'd never put myself in that situation again? Well, I fucking meant it. No love. Not ever. I'm steering myself far away from that shit."

Scarlett's hand slapped against the table. "You must have completely lost your mind because how in the hell can you say that you're not in love with Eve?"

"Because I'm not."

"You might not say the words to her," Scarlett added, "but you definitely feel it."

I shook my head.

"You can't be with someone for two years and not be in love with them," she added.

"I care about her."

"You love her," Brett said.

"I don't."

"Jesus fucking Christ," Jack said. "What Kristin did to you was fucked up, and it took you years to get over it, but look at you guys now. You're friends. You've had dinner together, and you're able to hang out and not feel the resentment you once did."

I listened to what each of them had said.

But it changed nothing.

"I wish Eve didn't want more," I said. "I wish she were satisfied with the way things were. They were so fucking perfect, and she had to go and ruin it all." I heard a laugh and followed the sound over to Brett. "What's so fucking funny?" I snapped.

Brett pushed his chair away from the table and crossed a leg over his thigh. "Do you remember the conversation we had about this? When I told you that you and Eve had been playing this game for too long? That the trips she made to Miami every few weeks would get old, and she'd get tired of it and want to get married one day? I knew she'd kick it into high gear once James started talking about our wedding, and it looks like I was right."

"So, you're saying I should have expected this?"

"I'm saying, you're being a fucking idiot, and you need to give that girl what she wants."

"Fuck this." I stood and paced the length of the conference room and back. "I gave her everything I'm capable of."

"No, you didn't," Scarlett said. "Because, when I compare what you gave to Kristin to what you gave to Eve, Eve got the short end of that stick."

I stopped walking and stared at her.

"And I mean very short, barely even a twig."

I grabbed the back of an empty chair and clenched my fingers around the leather cushion. "What the fuck, you guys? Why don't you tell me how you really feel?"

"Max, I'm glad you said that because I'm going to right now," Scarlett said. "As a woman, I would prefer my man to be in the same state as me. I'd like him to make as much effort as I was making. I'd like us to be on the same page as far as marriage and children. And you and Eve weren't at all. If I were her, I would have dumped your ass a long time ago."

I stopped grinding my hands over the leather and fixed my gaze on her. "I won't tell her not to take the job, so there's no point in even discussing this. I also won't tell her to put her dreams on hold. I'm not that guy, and I won't ever be."

"Then, be the kind of guy she wants when she comes back from Italy."

I wanted to fucking laugh. "And how am I supposed to do that? She broke up with me. We're done. I don't even know when she's leaving for Italy. Besides, she's asking for things I can't give her."

"There's someone in this room who can easily find out when she's leaving." Scarlett glanced at Brett before she looked back at me. "And they are things you can give her. You're just too stubborn and scared and extremely scarred."

"Scarlett—"

"Max, you need to make this right," she said, cutting me off. "Because, if you lose her like you lost Kristin, I know you'll regret it for the rest of your life."

I didn't want to lose Eve.

Scarlett was right about that.

But what the fuck would I say to her? How could I make this right?

I calmed myself down and finally said, "I want to be with her."

"You need to tell her that," Brett said.

The only way to do that was to go to her house. Beg her to fucking talk to me and tell her how much I cared about her before I flew out tomorrow morning.

"I'm going to go see her when we're done," I told the three of them.

"Good. I'm happy to hear that." Scarlett took her arms off the table and sat up higher. "Now that we have you and Eve figured out, we have to come to a conclusion about the partnership because the three partners from Entertainment Management Worldwide will be here in an hour to meet us, and we need to at least be open to hearing what they have to say." She looked at the other side of the table where Brett and Jack were sitting. "Have the two of you reviewed the contract?"

"Yes," Brett said. "I've read it in its entirety, and I've highlighted my concerns and a few items that need to be negotiated. But, overall, I'm pleased with the terms."

"And?" Scarlett said.

"And I've thought long and hard about this partnership, and I think it will benefit our business. I want to meet the partners first. Assuming we like them, I don't have an issue with having three more chiefs. We all will have our territories, so I don't see that as being a problem."

"Same here," Jack said, wrapping his hands around his coffee cup. "I found the contract to be surprisingly solid. I found just a few issues, but I don't anticipate any problems on either side. As long as we can make it a smooth transition and we get a good feeling from the guys, I think this is a done deal."

Everyone's stare shifted over to me.

"I didn't have time to read the contract, so I had our in-house counsel send me the main points, and I briefly reviewed them."

"What do you think?" Scarlett asked.

"Let's meet the guys. I'll read the contract during my flight tomorrow, and I'll give you an answer in a few days."

"That's fair." She picked up the phone sitting by her on the table and pressed a button on the keypad. "It's Scarlett in the conference room. Can you run out and get a bagel sandwich with a fried egg, lots of cheese, and make sure it's extra greasy? I also need the largest coffee you can find." She paused. "Come back as quickly as you can. Thank you."

"Man, I hope that's for me," I said, my stomach growling from the description.

I didn't remember eating at the opening last night, and I knew I hadn't this morning. The only thing that was in my body was liquor, and there was a hell of a lot of it in there.

"Well, it's certainly not for me." She laughed. "The grease will sober you up a little and hopefully put some color back in your cheeks."

"You need it," Jack said. "You look like shit."

I flipped him off. "Thanks, dickhead."

Scarlett got up and walked over to me. "This is an important meeting, Max. I need you at your best. So, here's what I want you to do." She put her hand on my back and walked me toward the door. "Go into our office and make use of that big leather couch. I'll bring in the bagel when it gets delivered." When we got to the door, she opened it and led me through it. "A power nap will do wonders for you right now."

I gave her a weak smile. "That makes up for the ass chewing you just gave me."

She smiled back and shut the door behind her, so I headed down the hallway toward the executive offices, the same fucking place where Eve had ended things last night. As I passed the window where I'd found her standing, I remembered the way she had looked at me. Her eyes had been so goddamn hard, but when I'd kissed her, she had pushed her body into me.

All it would take was a few promises, and I could have her body pressing against mine again, I could have her lips waiting for me, I could have her legs spread.

I could have her forever.

This was a fucking mess.

Once I was inside our office, I took off my jacket and rested it over the back of the chair. My tie was next, and then I slid my phone out of my pocket and sat on the couch. I opened the last message I'd sent Eve and started typing.

Me: I'm flying out in the morning, and I want to see you before I leave.

Me: I just want to talk.

Me: Hear me out, Eve. Please.

TWENTY-FIVE
MAX

SHANE WALKER PUSHED his body to the end of the couch and cleared his throat. In a drunken voice, he said, "Listen to me, you guys. If the seven of us partnered up, we'd do some serious damage in this industry. Anyone who is anyone will want to sign with us."

Shane was one of the partners at Entertainment Management Worldwide. He focused solely on musicians and oversaw that department for their company.

"Fuck yeah, we would," Blake Dion said, holding his scotch in the air. "I'll cheers to that."

Blake was their second partner, and he managed athletes. Jayson Brady was the third, and he worked with actors. They each had a large team of managers beneath them, the same way the three of us had teams of agents who worked underneath us, and they were spread out across their bicoastal offices.

With Blake's glass still high in the air, we all raised ours and clinked them together.

By the way today had gone down, I'd say my friends were more than fucking excited to get that contract signed.

After my short nap, Shane, Blake, and Jayson had come to our office, and we'd ended up chatting all afternoon, discussing their business, the model they adhered to, their processes, and revenue. Once the meeting wrapped up, we all had gone for dinner, and now, we were in the VIP room of a club in West Hollywood with a table full of booze.

The four of us certainly hadn't planned on spending this much time with them, but we'd gotten along so well that no one seemed to be in a rush to end the night.

"We're not just going to do serious damage," Brett said, scotch sloshing out of the top of his glass. "We're going to dominate South Florida, LA, and Manhattan—all the major markets."

"Don't set your sights so low," Blake said. "We're going to take over Atlanta, Vegas, and Denver, too. And then we'll expand into London, Shanghai, and Dubai. We'll call it The Agency and Management Worldwide."

"God, that's fucking sexy," Jack said.

"It sure as hell is," I agreed.

Expansion meant more growth. More clients. More services that we could provide and therefore more revenue. And, with business exploding the way it was, especially in our music division, I saw the need for everything this partnership could provide.

Now, I just needed more time to take on all the clients who wanted to sign with me. I was so booked out, I'd been passing them down to my team and then overseeing those agents to make sure they were giving our musicians everything they needed.

I gave this job everything I fucking had.

And that meant Eve had never gotten all of me.

Goddamn it.

As I looked up, Shane stood from the couch, grabbing one of the bottles off the table, enough glasses for all of us, and he filled each one halfway. Then, he handed them out to all of us and said,

"To our future, together, as one big fucking company. The Agency and Management. Let's fucking do this."

"To our future," Scarlett said, "once the seven of us sign."

Always the voice of goddamn reason.

"To our future once the seven of us sign," Shane clarified. "And taking over the fucking agent and management world."

"Now, I like the sound of that," Scarlett said.

I raised my glass in the air, knowing more alcohol was the last thing I needed, and then I shot it down my throat. Whatever it was burned like hell as I swallowed, and I chased it with a beer that I'd found on the table.

As I put both glasses down, my phone vibrated in my pocket. I quickly pulled it out and saw that it was a text from a client.

Even through this haze of booze, I still felt the disappointment that it wasn't Eve's name on the screen.

I'd texted her several other messages besides the ones I'd sent from our office, and she hadn't responded to any of them. I'd even called her when we were on our way to the club, and she hadn't answered.

"Are you all right?" Scarlett asked, leaning into my side.

I knew she was looking at my phone to see whom the message was from.

I typed a quick reply and put my cell back in my pocket. "I haven't heard from her."

"Do you know where she is?"

I shook my head. "No fucking idea."

"We're flying out at nine tomorrow morning." She looked at her Rolex. "And it's almost midnight."

"Are you telling me I should get out of here and go to her place?"

"That's exactly what I'm telling you." She nodded toward the group. "At this point, it's just alcohol-induced banter. You're not going to miss anything."

If the boss was giving me permission to leave, I needed to fucking take it.

I brushed a kiss over her cheek, and then I stood from the couch and said, "I'm out, guys." I clasped hands with Brett and Jack. "I'll see you two on the plane tomorrow." Then, I man-hugged Jayson, Blake, and Shane. "It was real good to meet you three."

"You, too, man," one of them said.

"We'll be seeing more of you very soon," another one responded.

"I don't doubt it," I replied, and I made my way to the front of the club.

Our driver was parked along the side of the building, and when I reached his SUV, I pounded my fist against the glass to get his attention. He unlocked the door, and I got into the backseat and gave him Eve's address.

While he drove, I tried calling her again. After four rings, it went to her voice mail.

I hoped to hell that just meant she was sleeping.

I would find out that answer shortly because it didn't take long for us to arrive at her place. The driver pulled up in front of her house and came to a stop.

"Would you like me to wait for you?" he asked.

"Nah. You can head back to the club. The others will need a ride soon."

I climbed out and went to the front door, taking out my set of keys to open it. Fortunately, she hadn't changed the locks, and the key slid right in.

Once I was inside, I flipped on the lights and saw how different everything looked. It was usually covered in clothes and shoes and all the other shit women wore. Now, the couch had been moved out, everything had been organized into racks and built-ins, and the room had been transformed into a goddamn closet.

It was a sign that she wasn't going to be living here for the next six months.

One that made me fucking crazy.

I continued into the hallway, trying to be quiet as I entered her bedroom. I wasn't more than a few steps in when I saw that her bed was empty. I checked her bathroom, but I knew before I even turned on the light that she wasn't in there.

Fuck.

With no place to sit in the living room, I decided that getting in bed was the only option. So, I ditched my clothes and climbed under the covers.

I tried calling her one last time, and all I got was her voice mail. I followed that with a text that asked where she was. I knew I wouldn't get a response, so I dragged her pillow across the bed and buried my face in it.

It smelled just like her.

Oranges and fall fucking leaves.

Goddamn it, I just wanted to talk to her, to be in her presence, to graze my fingers across the softness of her skin.

But she wasn't giving me that chance.

She'd completely shut me out, and I had no way to reach her.

I put my phone down right next to me, and I closed my eyes.

I wasn't sure when I had fallen asleep, but a loud beeping noise woke me. My lids popped open, and I saw that it was my cell. I grabbed it off the mattress and turned off my alarm, and then I looked across the bed.

The spot next to me was empty.

I sighed, dragging my ass out of the covers, and went into the bathroom to take a piss and brush my teeth. When I came out, I got dressed and checked all the rooms to make sure she wasn't sleeping in one of them.

Of course she fucking wasn't.

So, I called the company the partners and I used to transport us around LA and told them I needed a ride to the airport, and then I went into the kitchen. I found a piece of paper and a pen, and I sat down to write her a note.

I waited for you all night.
I wish you had come home.
All I wanted was to talk to you, to see you one last time before you left for Italy.
Baby, don't do this—to me, to us.
You know how much I care about you.
Call me.
—Max

TWENTY-SIX
EVE

EXACTLY TWENTY DAYS had passed since I accepted Alberto's offer. During that time, I'd gotten Trevor comfortable with all of his responsibilities, we'd established a schedule of how often we'd be video-conferencing and the logistics of those meetings, and we'd converted my house into the office where he'd work. I'd also met with each of my clients and explained our new process. I'd still be styling them; the only difference was that Trevor would deliver the clothes that I chose, and he'd be conducting the fittings.

Professionally, everything was coming together perfectly. All the items I had shipped to Italy—my clothes, cosmetics, and things I needed for work—had arrived and were waiting for me in my apartment. And, as long as the internet connection was strong in Milan, like Alberto had promised it would be, I'd be able to run my business seamlessly.

But, personally, my life was a fucking disaster.

After I'd left Max at the soft opening, I'd checked into a hotel, and I hadn't returned home until I knew he was on his plane, flying out of California.

I couldn't see him.

I just wasn't strong enough for that.

If I were in his presence again, the love I had for him would control my words, my actions, and I knew I wouldn't be as strong the second time around.

I couldn't take that risk.

Because, if I gave in, if I let him touch my body or sweet-talk me, nothing would change between us.

I would still want more.

He would still deny me of it.

And I would end up leaving for Italy even more upset than I already was.

So, I didn't answer his phone calls, and I didn't return his texts.

But I listened to every voice mail he'd left, and I read every message he'd sent. Even though they wrecked my emotions, they made me feel close to him. They warmed the emptiness I felt inside my chest. They kept me from having an emotional breakdown as the realization of what our future looked like really took shape in my mind.

And then, three days ago, I hadn't been able to control myself.

I just got home after working a sixteen-hour day. I was completely exhausted. I went straight to the fridge and poured myself an extra-large glass of wine, and I brought it over to the table and sat down.

The first thing my eyes landed on was the note Max had left.

I'd read it before.

In fact, I knew every word by heart.

So much so that I could close my eyes and see the straightness of his letters, the spots where he had pushed a little harder with the pen.

And, while I read it again, I sipped from my glass, each line sending me another memory.

Ones that had his hands on my body.

Ones that had his mouth on my pussy.

Ones that had his dick thrusting inside me.

God, that fucking cock.

When the glass was empty and my hand was no longer holding it, my fingers began to crawl down the front of me where they unbuttoned my pants and dived under my panties.

I was already wet.

Swollen.

Ready for the friction, I hoped it would give my body the release I needed.

Each movement of my hand caused the scene in my head to shift. I wasn't just thinking of Max. I was seeing him. I was feeling him. I was watching him drop two fingers down my folds and insert them inside me while he pressed his palm against my clit.

My head fell back, rounding the top of the chair.

My mouth opened, a moan falling through my lips.

He was relentlessly plunging those fingers, and it felt so good.

I was so turned on, so ready, that I could hear him slide through my wetness.

And I could see it on his cock because, as I looked down, he was now using his dick to drive in and out of me. He pumped hard, fast, deep, his hand grinding my clit so that the build would immediately come.

I groaned his name, squeezing the side of the chair as leverage as the intensity completely took over my body.

His mouth was on my neck. His breath was panting over my face.

He was using all the strength he had to pound out our orgasms, and I screamed in response.

As I hit the peak, my stomach shuddered, and my limbs turned numb. I stopped breathing, and every nerve began to pulse, the sensation of sparks moving through me.

It took me a while to calm. When I did, my eyes flicked open.

That was when I saw my real surroundings.

I was sitting at my kitchen table with Max's note in front of me and my fingers buried deep inside me.

But I wished it had been him.

In the haze that I found myself in, I had a moment of weakness, and I decided to give him one more chance.

So, I found my phone, and I called the airline that I was taking to Italy. When the customer service representative asked what she could help me with, I told her I wanted to change my flights.

I loved this man, and I needed to tell him.

And I was about to get the opportunity because, now, I was sitting in the back of an SUV after having just landed at the Miami airport, and I was on my way to Max's house.

I hadn't told him I was coming, and I still hadn't replied to any of his messages.

The only reason I knew he was in town was because I'd had James do a little snooping.

There was a chance he wouldn't be home or that he wouldn't return until really late tonight.

I didn't care.

I just needed to talk to him, to get these things off my chest before I got on the plane to Italy. Saying it to his face was the only way to do it, and I believed surprising him was the best approach.

When the SUV pulled up to the side of Max's gate, I said to the driver, "You can let me off here."

"Would you like me to wait?" he asked.

"No need, but thank you."

I handed him a cash tip and went up to the call box, pressing the buttons that would open the gate. Once there was enough space for me to slip through, I made my way up the driveway and over to the back door where there was a keypad. I entered my six-digit code and walked inside.

I got as far as the entrance to the kitchen, and that was when I heard Max's voice.

"Are you sure about this?" he said.

There was no way he knew I was here; therefore, I knew he wasn't speaking to me.

"Yes, Max," I heard a woman say.

Hearing her made my feet halt, the blood slowly draining from my face.

In the last two years, I'd never known Max to have a woman at his house.

So, what is she doing here? At almost eight o'clock at night?

And who the hell is she?

My hands started to shake as I made my way to the back side of the kitchen. The flats I wore were silent as I stepped across the hardwood floor. I didn't even take a breath until I reached the last row of cabinets, gripping the edge of the counter as I peered into the living room.

The sight before me almost had the two glasses of wine I'd sipped on the plane come purging out of my mouth.

And it took everything I had not to make a sound.

Max was on the couch, his legs extended and crossed over the ottoman. One arm was spread across the back of the cushions while the other was bent with his cheek resting on his hand. He had a grin on his face.

A grin I'd thought he reserved only for me.

But I was wrong.

Because someone else was causing him to smile that way.

That someone was sitting directly next to him with her body facing his.

And that someone was Kristin fucking Evans.

His ex.

"I've wanted to do this for a long time," she said. "I just didn't have the courage."

"What changed?" he asked.

I was squeezing the counter so hard; I was sure every nail was going to break off.

"You," she said. "After we hung out at the bar in LA the night of James's premiere, I started planning my future, and it all centered around you."

The night of James's premiere?

But he had met me that night at the after-party.

Except he had been late.

Extremely fucking late, and I'd wondered what had taken him so long to arrive.

Now, I knew that answer.

And, on top of their little date at the bar, he'd had dinner with her in Miami.

All while we'd been together.

Two occasions he'd conveniently forgotten to tell me about.

Because he must have had something to hide.

I was definitely going to be sick.

Oh God, I hadn't thought my heart could hurt worse than the night I had broken up with him.

I'd been so wrong.

I hated myself for not talking to him about Kristin. I'd been such an emotional mess over our relationship, stressing about the things he wasn't willing to give me, that I'd never confronted him about the dinner James had told me about.

Yet I'd had every opportunity to do so.

Not that it mattered anymore. It was clear what was going on between them.

Even more so now that Max's smile had grown larger, and he was laughing at Kristin's last statement.

My body turned even tighter, my stomach churning as I watched the two of them.

Part of me wanted to scream in his face.

The other part wanted to fall on his kitchen floor and cry.

But, if I walked into that living room the way I wanted to, calling him a piece of shit and the most disgusting man on the fucking planet, it would make me look like a jealous, psycho bitch. Because, technically, he had every right to do what he was doing.

I'd ended our relationship. I hadn't answered any of his calls. I hadn't responded to his texts.

He had moved on.

I just couldn't believe it had happened so soon.

And I couldn't believe he had chosen to do it with her.

Seeing the way she looked at him made my skin crawl.

But seeing the way he looked at her was torture.

The ache that filled my body was unbearable.

I couldn't watch this.

Not for another second.

So, I turned around and quietly walked through his kitchen. I went out the back door and down his driveway. Once I made it through his gate, I moved past the opening and to the side of the concrete fence and took a seat on the grass.

With my phone in my hand, I ordered a car to come pick me up. Since my flight to Italy wasn't until tomorrow evening, I needed somewhere to stay, so I found a hotel by the airport and booked a room for the night.

When I'd changed my flight, I never thought I'd have to do

any of this. I'd pictured Max and me talking through the night, finding my way into his arms, having sex until the moment I had to leave. I'd assumed I would use all of his cosmetics, so I hadn't brought any of my own, and I'd wear the clothes I'd put in my bag.

I'd thought we'd be in a better place.

I'd thought we'd be able to work things out.

I'd thought we'd have a future.

But the only person he had a future with was Kristin Evans.

God, why the hell did I come all the way here?

Why didn't I just leave things the way they were?

I'd broken up with him for a reason, and it wasn't a simple one. *What had made me think a conversation with him would change that, would get him to be the man I wanted him to be, would get me* more *when he'd told me that he wouldn't give it to me?*

For weeks, the last vision I'd had of him was the hurt on his face when I left him at the soft opening.

Now, all I could see was the grin that he'd given to Kristin.

And it made me want to scream.

But, before I even had the chance to open my mouth, I felt my phone vibrate in my hand, and the screen showed a text from James.

She was the only person who knew I had changed my flight.

If I told her what I'd just walked in on, she would get so angry that I knew she'd say something to Max. I didn't want that to happen, and I didn't want Max to know what I had done or what I had seen.

I didn't want to lie.

But I had no choice.

James: Is he home? Are you talking to him? Gah, I'm dying over here. I need to know what's going on with you two.

Me: Nothing is going on because I decided not to come. So, I changed my flight...again.

James: What? Why? You were so sure that talking to him was the right thing for you guys.

Me: I thought about it more and decided things are best the way they are now. I'm leaving for a long time. No need to make either of us wait. Besides, what if I meet a deliciously handsome Italian man, and I don't want to keep my hands off of him?

My eyes filled with tears as I sent the last message.

I couldn't even imagine putting my hands on another guy. Not when my heart was still with Max. Not when he was the man I wanted to spend the rest of my life with.

James: I'm sure there are going to be hundreds of deliciously handsome Italian men, but none of them are going to measure up to Max. We both know this. You love that man. I wish you had told him.

She knew me too well.

I should have known I wouldn't be able to fool her.

Still, she'd never know that I'd come to Miami, and that was what was important.

Me: Maybe, one day, we'll be together again. But telling him before I leave doesn't feel like the right time.

James: Stubborn bitch. Text me when you land. Love you.

"Eve Kennedy?" the driver said as he pulled up to where I was sitting with his window rolled down.

"Yep." I wiped my face. "That's me."

"Where am I taking you?"

I climbed in the back of the car, and as I told him the name of the hotel and the address, he pulled a U-turn in the middle of the road.

I stared at Max's front gate as we passed it.

I studied every detail.

I closed my eyes, my lids still dripping, to make sure I'd memorized it all.

I'd thought, one day, our vacation home would be behind that gate.

Now, in my memory was the only time I'd ever see it again.

TWENTY-SEVEN
MAX

Me: I fucking miss you.
UNDELIVERED.

I STARED at the message that appeared right under my text to Eve, a word that I'd never seen come through before.

What the fuck does undelivered mean?

I was sure it was a mistake, so I tried sending another text.

Me: I wish you would call me back.
UNDELIVERED.

She had to be in a location that had poor cell service, and her texts just weren't coming through.

But, just to make sure, I found her number in my Contacts, pressed the phone icon, and waited for it to start ringing.

Except it never fucking rang.

A recorded message began to play that said the number had been disconnected.

Because Eve used the same phone for business and personal calls, I couldn't believe that she would disconnect it, especially since she was already in Italy.

If this was more than an accident, asking James wouldn't get me anywhere. That girl would go to the grave before she told me a goddamn thing.

So, the only other option I had was to send Eve an email.

While I was already sitting at my desk, I shook the mouse to wake up my computer. I opened a new email, and I started typing.

With your phone shut off, it's even harder to get in touch with you.

Hopefully, it's just a mistake, and it will be turned back on soon.

Either way, I'm not giving up.

At least email me back, Eve, so I know you're all right.

Just as the email cleared my inbox, my cell began to ring.

"Kristin," I said as I answered.

"Hey, you. Have you given what we talked about any more thought?"

I laughed, swiveling back and forth in my chair as I looked out the window into downtown Miami. "It's only been two days since I saw you."

"And?"

"I need more time than that."

"Max, I'm extremely impatient. You know this about me."

I gripped the top of the Windsor knot and loosened it around my throat. "Listen to me, Kristin. I don't move fast when it comes to things like this, so get yourself some patience because you're not going to get an answer for at least a week."

"Ugh."

"Don't sound so upset. Your pitch was all right. This phone call serves as your follow-through. I'd say you have a decent shot at getting what you want."

She fucking giggled, and it reminded me of the sound she used to make when I tickled her. I used to love when she made that noise.

"That does make me feel a tiny bit better." She paused. "Hey, do you have plans for lunch? There's something I want to show you."

I turned back toward my computer and pulled up my calendar. "I can probably squeeze in an hour around two this afternoon."

"Perfect. I'll pick you up at your office."

"I'll see you then," I said and hung up.

I was just setting my cell back on my desk when I saw a reply from Eve come through my inbox.

It was about fucking time she responded to me.

I clicked on the email, and it enlarged on my screen.

Mr. Graham,
I'm Eve's assistant, Trevor, and while she's working overseas, I'm responsible for monitoring her email.
I'll be sure to pass along your message.

In the meantime, is there anything I can help you with?

Thanks!
Trevor Jackson
Assistant to Eve Kennedy

I slammed my finger onto the mouse, the email immediately getting deleted, and I walked over to the bar that was in the far side of my office. I found the scotch in the middle of all the other bottles, and I poured myself a finger's worth. The tumbler went straight to my lips, and I shot the booze down my throat.

It fucking burned.

And I wanted it to.

While I was setting the glass onto the counter to pour a little more, my office door opened, and Scarlett walked in. She stood halfway between my desk and the bar, and she put a hand on her goddamn hip.

"Do you want to talk about it?"

I shook my head, letting a few more drops fall from the bottle before I brought the glass to my lips again. Once I swallowed it all, I said, "Nah. It's nothing this scotch can't fix."

"For some reason, I doubt that." She waited for me to walk back to my desk before she added, "I have a hunch your day-drinking has to do with Eve."

I took a seat, running both hands through my hair. "I'm talked out, Scarlett. Besides, I've already told you everything. I spent the night at her place, and she never showed up. I call her every goddamn day, and she never answers. I text her more than that, and she doesn't reply. Today, I found out her phone is shut off, and her assistant—some fucking dude I didn't even know she'd hired—is monitoring her email, so I can't get in touch with her. No matter how hard I try, it's over between us."

"And you're okay with that?"

I dropped my fist onto my desk, and the stack of papers right next to it jumped into the air before they scattered. "Hell no, I'm not okay with it. But I don't know how to make this shit better, so I'm going to give her some time. That's obviously what she wants."

"Have you tried talking to James?"

I sighed so fucking loud, she knew my answer.

"I figured that was a long shot, but it was worth a mention." She took the seat across from me. "The good news is, Brett and James's wedding is in exactly six months, and Eve is the maid of honor, so you know you'll see her there."

I ground my teeth together. "That's what you consider good fucking news? Six months is an eternity from now."

"It is, but it gives you some time."

"For what?"

She wrapped her hands around the armrest and smiled. "To figure out how to give that girl what she wants."

"Jesus, Scarlett, you're relentless when it comes to that."

"That's because it's the only way you're going to get her back. I can promise you one thing, Max. She doesn't want to return to the same man she left. She had that, and look where it got you. She wants to come home to a better version of you."

I pushed back in my chair and crossed a leg over my knee. "So, you're saying, I have to change?"

"I'm saying, you have to meet her halfway, and if you love her, you will. The longer she's away, the more you're going to miss her, and the more obvious your love is going to be."

I laughed. "You're wrong."

"Oh no, my friend, I'm absolutely right. But we'll see, won't we?"

"I need another fucking drink."

"Not yet. We have to talk business first." She took a folder off her lap and put it on my desk. "Here's all the paperwork for the partnership. They came back and accepted our latest round of changes, so their attorney drew up a new contract. I need you to review it, and we'll discuss it as a team again. Then, we'll meet with our attorney to get it all wrapped up."

It had to be over a hundred pages thick.

"Now that you're single, you'll have plenty of time to read it."

I looked up from the stack. "Get out, wiseass."

"Drinks tonight?"

"If I'm not already tanked, yeah, drinks sound real good."

She smiled as she left my office, and I went back to the bar to pour myself another scotch.

TWENTY-EIGHT
EVE

ITALY WAS everything I'd imagined.

Intensely beautiful.

Quietly romantic.

Poetically charming.

I couldn't get enough of the landscape or the food. I couldn't take in enough of the culture and the accents and the smell that could only be described as warm citrus.

I loved it here.

More than I'd thought I would.

And I'd wanted it to be my new beginning, which was why, on the day I'd landed and moved into my apartment, I'd called my cell phone carrier and changed my number. I had known I didn't have to go to that extreme, and I could just block Max, but I needed fresh, and a new number had given me that.

Even though James or Trevor would never give it to him, there was still a chance Max could get my new digits. Still, I was willing to take that chance just to give myself a break from seeing his words and listening to his voice every day.

If that continued, there was no way I would ever move on.

But just because I'd stopped hearing from him didn't mean I'd stopped thinking about him.

That was the problem with having access to social media. I could never really escape. Pictures of him were only a click away, and I looked at them.

Way too often.

I saved those moments for late at night when I finally crawled into bed, knowing he was probably just waking up. When I got under the thin sheet and hugged a pillow to my chest, I wondered if his arms had been around another woman last night or if he had slept alone, if he had thought of me, if his heart was having a rough time healing.

I wondered if things were heating up between him and Kristin.

I was just waiting for the day when he posted a picture of the two of them online. It hadn't happened yet, but I was trying to prepare myself for it.

Besides what I had seen at his house, maybe what I needed was proof that he had moved on.

Maybe that was what it would take for me to finally heal.

I knew I could ask James to do some snooping, but I refused to put her in the middle. Plus, we'd made a promise not to discuss him. I just couldn't handle it.

Because what I really needed was to forget him, so I tried so hard to live my days unaffected by Max Graham.

I spent the first three hours of my morning at Horse Feathers' design studio where I worked with a team to create their new line. It was a process I had been unfamiliar with until I moved here. Their staff allowed me so much creative freedom. They listened to what I said. They trusted my opinion. They translated my words into stunning mock-ups even if they didn't initially believe the clothes would become something worth selling.

As soon as I left the studio around lunchtime, I would come

straight back to my apartment and look through the photos Trevor had sent the night before. His job was to visit the showrooms and pull items he thought I would like. Each piece was then photographed and categorized, and that was how I chose my clients' outfits. The items I picked would then be taken to the client's house, and more pictures would be shot, so I could see how they looked.

The system was working.

My clients were happy.

Trevor was in love with his job.

From the outside, it looked like everything was going perfectly. I guessed, in a way, it was.

I had what I'd always wanted—a loyal client base who supported my sixth-month hiatus; a business that was expanding, even with me being gone; an opportunity to gain knowledge from the other side of the industry, participating in a designer's line; and living abroad and experiencing a different culture like I never had before.

So, if I had everything, then why did nothing feel right?

Why did I go to bed with tears in my eyes?

When I'd met Alberto, he'd told me that their designs were influenced by their mood. They felt their surroundings and translated them into emotions, and each piece reflected that.

When I'd walked into their design studio for the first time four weeks ago, I'd told them that was something I didn't want to change.

This year's summer collection theme was going to be melancholy.

And, when the models put on the pieces and walked the runway in New York, Paris, and Rome, everyone would see the tears I'd shed over the love of my life.

TWENTY-NINE
MAX

"GOD, I'M SO FUCKING EXCITED," Kristin said from the passenger seat of my car.

She was wiggling against the leather, unable to sit still, turning her body toward me, then straight, and then to the right to look out the window.

I laughed at the way she was acting, especially because her excitement mostly had to do with me, which I thought was pretty sweet.

"You need to relax there, killer. The really good part hasn't even gone down yet."

She bent her knees and put her toes on the end of the seat. "I honestly don't know if I can wait, Max."

I smiled, turning toward her as I shifted into third. "You've waited this long."

"But it's been so hard. You're all calm and reserved, and I want so badly to act like you, but when I want something this much, I'm barely able to keep my hands off of it."

My grin grew. "Jesus, don't I know that."

There was that giggle again.

But I only heard it for a second before it got interrupted by the ringing of my phone, which came through the speakers in my car. The screen on the console showed it was James.

There was no fucking way I was going to talk to her on speakerphone in front of Kristin, so I sent her to voice mail.

"I'm sure that's a first," Kristin said.

I shifted into second, first, and then into neutral while I slowed for the red light. "What is?"

"That someone sends James Ryne to voice mail."

"I doubt that."

"She's the highest-paid actress, and everyone wants to work with her. She's stalked by the paparazzi and the envy of practically every woman in the world. But I'm sure you're probably right; most people just blow her off when she calls."

Before I had a chance to respond, the screen lit up again, and the ringing blasted from the speakers. I hit a button on the steering wheel that rejected the call.

I had no fucking idea what James wanted. She only phoned unless it had something to do with Brett or Eve. I couldn't imagine today was about the latter. And, since I'd just seen Brett at the office and he was going to be in meetings all day, I doubted anything was wrong with him.

Whatever she wanted could wait.

"Max, you know I understand how demanding your job is, so please don't avoid her call because of me."

I shifted into first when the light turned green and said, "It's all right. I'll call her back."

"Suit yourself." She traced her finger over the window, and after a few minutes of silence, she glanced at me. "How much of your time am I going to be lucky enough to get?" The excitement in her tone was gone. In its place was apprehension.

Her question reminded me of something Eve would have asked.

Something Scarlett would fucking lecture me about.

"Kristin, you know how busy I am."

"I know. That's why I'm asking. I need to know what I can expect from you."

The same thought had been on my mind during the last few times I saw her. I hadn't come up with a conclusion. With this new merger, I had a feeling I'd be working even more, traveling between all three offices until we found a process that worked for everyone.

"When I'm in town, I promise you'll get as much of me as I can swing."

Her smile was weak, but it was there. "I'll take whatever I can get, I guess." She turned her head straight, looking out the windshield, gripping and squeezing the top of her seat belt as it rested across her tits. "You know, when we were engaged and you were working for your old agency, you weren't as busy as you are now."

"That's because I have triple the client load."

"That's not even what I'm talking about." She put her feet down and tilted her body toward me, her face resting on the corner of the seat. "You were just more present. When I was with you, you listened to everything I said. I never had to repeat myself. You didn't look at your phone as much. You were able to relax and breathe, and I didn't feel like your brain was totally consumed with work."

"Why don't you tell me how you really fucking feel?"

"I'm being kind." Her tone softened. "The truth is much worse than what I'm describing."

I shook my head, baffled at how she could think I wouldn't have changed. "I own a goddamn business now. I have hundreds of agents working beneath me. We just built a second office, and we're merging with two more. I run a fucking empire, Kristin. My brain might be just a tad bit busy at times."

"I miss that guy. The old version of you, I mean."

I sighed, tired of everyone telling me how I needed to be and how I wasn't enough and the changes I had to make. If it wasn't Scarlett, then it was Eve, and now, it was Kristin.

I didn't understand why they couldn't accept me for who I was and just shut the fuck up about it.

I pulled into a parking spot in front of the high-rise building that Kristin and I were going into, and I turned off the car. That was when I felt a vibration in my pocket. I took out my phone, and James's name was on the screen.

Fucking Christ.

Before I opened the door, I turned toward Kristin and said, "Listen to me, the guy you're looking at is the same guy you knew back then. I'm just a hell of a lot busier now. I travel more, and I have too much shit going on in my head. If you're not feeling me, then maybe what we have going on here isn't a good idea."

She stared at me for several seconds, as though she were thinking about what I'd said. And then her lips finally parted. "You know it's everything I want." Her voice became so goddamn soft. "It's all I think about. Don't take that away from me."

I nodded toward her door, signaling for her to get out, and I did the same. Just as we were walking up to the building, my phone vibrated again.

I held the door open for her while I gazed at the screen.

James had called four times in five minutes.

Something was fucking wrong.

"Kristin—"

"Please just answer the call. I'll wait for you in the lobby."

She continued to walk inside, and I released my hold on the door handle.

Then, I pressed the screen to accept the call. "James—"

"Thank God you finally answered." She sounded so fucking panicked. "It's Eve, Max. She's been in an accident, and I didn't know who else to call."

My feet froze over the goddamn pavement.

Eve?

Has been in a fucking accident?

It felt like someone had just punched me in the fucking gut.

My hand went into my hair, and I pulled at the strands. "What the fuck are you talking about, James?"

"The hospital in Milan called me. I guess I'm listed as her in case of emergency. There was an accident. She was on a bike, and a van hit her."

"Oh, fuck no."

"It's bad, Max. They said she's hurt, and they're taking her straight in for surgery." There was so much fucking emotion in her voice. The only time I'd heard her this fucked up was in one of her movies. "I'm filming on location, and if I leave, I'll be in breach of my contract."

My brain was trying to keep up, but this was too much to process.

Eve was in a hospital, going into surgery.

We didn't know what was going to happen.

We didn't know what was wrong.

We only knew that it was bad.

She was over four thousand miles away.

She needed someone there.

That person was going to be me.

"I'm headed to the airport right now," I told her.

She let out a sob. "Max, I'm freaking out. I can't lose her. Do you hear me? I can't lose my best friend. She means everything to me. I don't know what they're doing to her or if she has a good doctor or—"

"James, take a breath and hear me out. I'm leaving for the airport right now, and I'm going to take care of everything."

"Okay."

"She's going to be fine."

I didn't know if that was true, but I had to fucking say it. And I had to fucking believe it because I didn't want to live in a world that didn't have Eve in it.

"You're going to take care of her," she repeated, like she needed to say it to convince herself, to calm herself down.

"I'll let you know the second I get there and I find out what's going on with her."

"Okay."

It took a lot to shake me.

But hearing that something had happened to Eve rocked me harder than when Kristin had called off our engagement.

"I'll text you the name of the hospital," she added.

"James?" I'd been pacing the front of the building, but I started to move back toward the entrance. "I won't let anything happen to her."

"I know."

I hung up and slid the phone into my pocket, and my eyes connected with Kristin's as she stared at me through the glass walls of the lobby.

I opened the door and said, "I have to go." I reached into my other pocket and took out my wallet, removing a hundred dollar bill that I handed to her. "I don't have time to take you back to your apartment, so use this to pay for a car service."

I released the door, turned around, and headed for my Aston Martin.

"Max!" I heard Kristin shout from behind me. "Where are you going?"

"I'll text you from the plane," I said over my shoulder, and I got into the driver's seat and drove straight to the airport.

THIRTY
EVE

THE FIRST THING I felt was warmth. It was in my chest, trickling down my arms and legs like little bursts of electricity. I'd never felt this toasty or this comfortable before. And it wasn't just a heat that was spreading but almost a happiness, too, that made the black behind my lids as pretty and as sparkly as the ocean.

I moved my toes, flexing them up and down, crossing the first two and then wiggling the rest.

I could tell there was stiffness in my ankles; I couldn't move them as fast as I wanted to. They didn't hurt. Not even a little. There was far too much hotness in my muscles for that.

"Eve," I heard.

It was a voice I recognized.

A voice that made me want to smile.

A voice I loved so much.

"Max." The voice that came out of me didn't sound like mine. It was hoarse and extra scratchy, and it made me think my throat should be sore. But it wasn't; I couldn't feel it.

What I did feel was my tongue. I swore, it was a hundred pounds.

"That's it, baby," he said. "Come back to me."

Come back?

But I hadn't left. I was right here, in this cozy cocoon.

"Open your eyes, Eve."

I knew they were closed.

I wasn't sure why.

And, when I tried to lift my lids, they felt as heavy as my tongue.

Maybe I just wasn't ready to wake up from this nap yet.

If it were a nap I had taken.

Surely, it was, and I'd just fallen asleep while I was tanning out in the sun.

"Can you open your eyes and look at me?"

I wanted to do what he'd asked, so I focused solely on them. My chest rose and fell so fast as I tried to lift my eyes. My toes twitched. And, with more effort than I thought it would take, they finally cracked.

A medium amount of light crept in.

Medium, like the blinds had been opened just a notch.

Not like the sun was sitting directly over me.

I pushed harder and got my eyes halfway open, my pupils burning from the air. I felt them water, and I blinked away the drops. And then I drove them up the rest of the way, taking in the first thing I saw.

It was Max.

He was standing over me. I saw concern. Sleepiness. I thought I saw fear.

"Hi." My voice was just as scratchy as it had been before, my tongue even heavier.

"Gorgeous girl, thank God you're awake," he whispered. "You scared the fuck out of me, you know that?" He bent down, and his mouth pressed against my forehead.

He kept it there.

The air he exhaled tickled the top of my head.

Each breath sent me more of his smell.

Leather and spice.

It was a beautiful scent, just like the blackness I'd seen that gleamed the same way as the ocean.

"You scared the fuck out of me."

But why?

How?

I'd just been napping under the sun. Or maybe it wasn't the sun because the light wasn't strong enough. Maybe this was his room. Or the couch.

Beep. Beep. Beep.

What is that noise?

Beep. Beep. Beep.

"Max?"

"Yes, baby."

"What's that sound?"

"It's your heart rate; it's being monitored."

"My...*what*?"

Max moved several inches back, his lips no longer touching me. "How do you feel?"

"I don't know." I turned my head, and a wave of exhaustion hit me.

But, with this new view, I saw that there were two windows to my right. A television was across from me. A white blanket was over me, and large, rectangular armrests were on each side of me. I turned my head to the other side and saw a machine. There was a pole, too, that had bags hanging from it.

This wasn't Max's bedroom.

This was a hospital room.

And the machine had wires coming out of it with round pads at the end that were attached to my chest. The bags that hung from the pole were hooked to a tube that was taped to my hand.

"Max..."

It was all starting to come back to me.

I was riding my bike to the store. I wanted a bottle of wine and some focaccia. I cycled down my cobblestone street and stopped where it forked.

I heard something behind me and looked over my shoulder.

It was a van.

I moved as far to the right as I could. I peddled faster. The street was so narrow, as most of them were, and it was squeezed between the back side of long residential buildings.

I slammed against one.

I bounced to the left as my body flew off the seat of the bike.

I hit the van.

I tasted the stone that I had fallen against.

Pain.

It was blinding.

There was screaming. Loud voices. Cries.

A pulse so intense, I felt it in my ears.

That was all I could remember.

And, now, I was here.

"Max..."

"I'm right here, baby."

Here?

Here was...Italy.

Milan.

A job I had accepted, designing Horse Feathers' new summer collection.

Here because Max hadn't asked me to stay.

He wouldn't give me the things I wanted.

More.

I'd broken up with him at the soft opening.

Then, I'd flown to Miami.

I'd wanted to tell him I loved him.

But Kristin. She was there.

I'd changed my phone number.

We were done.

Forever.

"Max..."

"Listen to me, Eve, your body has been through so much in the last two days. Waking up and talking to me have taken a lot out of you. I know you probably have so many questions, and I promise you'll get all those answers. But, right now, I want you to close your eyes again and go back to sleep. I've already alerted the nurse, and she'll be here any second."

There was gentleness.

On his face.

In his voice.

"But I—"

"Trust me, you need the rest. It's the only way you're going to heal."

Heal?

I looked down again and saw that my arm was in a cast. It went all the way to my shoulder and stopped at my wrist. And then there were the pads on my chest that were causing the machine to *beep, beep, beep.*

Is my heart okay?

Are other parts of me hurt?

What happened to me?

The beeping got louder, faster, and two women were suddenly standing over me. They were speaking in Italian.

I didn't know what they were saying.

"Max?"

"Eve, you need to relax and bring your heart rate down. Focus on your breathing, baby. Slow breaths—can you do that for me?"

Slow breaths.

Baby.

Baby?

There was more Italian. More faces staring at the machine. More movement. A syringe poked into the thing that was taped on my hand.

Warm.

There was so much more warmth.

And then there was darkness.

My eyes no longer felt like they weighed a hundred pounds. Maybe just half that weight, and they were extremely sensitive. Still, I was able to lift my lids without putting in every bit of strength I had.

When I finally got them open, I saw Max. He was sitting in a chair beside my bed, his arm extended over to me with his hand resting on top of mine. His eyes were closed, and I could tell he was sleeping.

It was darker in the room. The blinds were still open a crack, but the moon shone in instead of sunlight.

Time had passed.

I just wasn't sure how much.

"Hi," I whispered.

His lids flicked open, and his stare caught mine. He immediately leaned forward in his chair, so he could get closer to me. "The nurse gave you something to knock you out. She was concerned you'd start to panic and rip out your drain."

"My drain?"

With his other hand, he brushed the hair out of my face. Once all the strands were moved, he continued to stroke my cheek. "You punctured your lung, and they had to surgically repair it. You have a drain in until tomorrow."

"What else is wrong with me?"

"Several broken ribs, a tear in your shoulder, fractured wrist, elbow, and humerus. They repaired your arm during surgery, and you now have several pins holding it together."

"Oh my God."

"You're going to be fine." He squeezed my hand. "I've had every fucking doctor who has walked through your door assure me of that."

The worry had worn on him. He seemed as exhausted as me.

He looked soft.

I'd never seen him appear that way before.

"How did you get here?"

He rested his chin on the armrest that was only a foot away from me. "James called me when she found out you were in an accident. She couldn't come because she's filming, but she might as well be here. She calls every ten minutes."

I laughed, and a scorching hot, burning sensation seared across the sides of my stomach.

I pulled my hand away from his to put pressure on the places that hurt.

"It's your ribs," he said. "They're going to take a while to heal, and there's nothing they can give you to speed it up. I've asked, trust me. But you're on an IV pain med, and I can tell them to up the drip if you need it."

"No." I could feel the pain med in my system. I was sure it was the warmth that pulsed through my body and the fuzziness in my head. "I don't want any more drugs."

"I don't want you to be in pain."

I could handle the hurt in my ribs. It was minimal compared

to how bad it could be, and I was sure the meds were the reason I was able to tolerate it.

The real pain came from the man sitting next to me.

"Why are you here?"

"James called me—"

"No, Max. Why are you really here?"

It took him several seconds to respond. "When I heard you were injured and in the hospital, there wasn't anywhere else I wanted to be."

"Why?"

"Because I care about you. You know that. I've been saying that to you for years."

I licked the inside of my lips, feeling how dry and cracked they were, not knowing the last time any water had touched them. "Tell me something, Max. Tell me something I want to hear."

His hand was still on me even though I'd pulled mine away. He moved his down my leg, stopping mid-thigh. "When I thought I might lose you, I lost my fucking mind. I screamed at every goddamn person in this hospital until I got the answer I wanted to hear."

Disappointment washed through as fast as these meds were pumping through my veins.

"That's all you've got?" I asked him, hearing my voice crack.

He shook his head, his eyes wide, his lids red with tiredness. "What do you want from me, Eve?"

I'd answered that question.

Too many fucking times.

I'd thought the reason he was here was because he wanted the same things I did.

But nothing had changed.

He still wouldn't tell me he loved me.

He wouldn't tell me he'd move to LA.

He wouldn't tell me he would give me more.

He was worried he would lose me, but he'd already lost me. And, in this bed, I'd given him a chance to get me back.

He hadn't taken it.

So, I no longer needed his hand to squeeze.

I no longer needed him to talk to the medical staff.

I was awake.

I could do it.

"I'd like you to leave."

His brows rose, and he laughed. "Stop it. You're in the fucking hospital. I'm not leaving you—"

"Max, now, you need to listen to me." I took a breath, and I knew the tightness wasn't just because my lung had been punctured. "I appreciate you coming here and staying with me while I was out of it. But I'm stronger now, and I don't need you here anymore."

"Why are you doing this?"

The image of him smiling with Kristin on his couch flashed through my head. I forced it out and took another breath, the burning in my ribs reminding me not to inhale so deep. "I broke up with you for a reason. Being in the hospital doesn't change that."

"Eve—"

"Don't make me ask you again, or I'll call the nurse and tell her to have security escort you out of my room."

I hated the way he was looking at me.

I hated that I had to be such a bitch to him.

I hated that he had disappointed me again.

I hated that the pain in my heart had returned, that I'd made it six weeks in Italy, and seeing him felt like I was starting all over.

"Get out."

I turned my head in the opposite direction and rested my cheek on the pillow.

I closed my eyes.

I felt the emptiness when his hand lifted off my leg, and I felt the hollowness in my body when the door to my room closed.

I didn't open my eyes when he was gone. I didn't want to see the chair next to me vacant.

So, I kept them shut, even when the wetness dripped from them.

And they stayed that way until a nurse came in and asked how I felt.

I looked at her and said, "Broken." I pointed at the left side of my chest. "It hurts in here."

But I knew there wasn't any medicine she could put in my IV that would make that part of my body feel better.

THIRTY-ONE
MAX

I STOOD in front of the mirror in the employee restroom and used both hands to straighten my tie. Once I was satisfied with the knot, I checked my hair and ran my palms over my trimmed beard.

I was tired.

And it showed.

It had been a long two and a half months since I returned from Italy. I remembered the call I'd made to James when I left the hospital and was on my way to the goddamn airport. She'd said nothing; she'd just listened while I gave her the highlights of what had just gone down. Before I'd hung up, I had given her Eve's room number, and I'd told her not to let a fucking thing happen to her.

I hadn't seen James since, and I hadn't spoken to her.

I hadn't asked anyone for an update on Eve.

That would be changing tonight.

And I was fucking ready for it.

"You look handsome," Kristin said, her voice causing me to get out of my head.

I turned toward the door and saw her leaning against the frame. Her arms were crossed over her chest, the baggy sleeves of her white double-breasted jacket bulking around her.

"Thanks," I replied.

She tilted her head to the side and really took me in. "Don't tell me you're nervous."

I brushed the last few whiskers forward and walked out with her right next to me. "I don't get nervous."

She slowed in the hallway and came to a stop. "Well, just because you're not doesn't mean I feel the same way." She took a long, deep breath, and I could tell it wasn't easy for her. "Max, I'm freaking out right now."

All the time we'd spent together at my house.

All the meetings we'd had at my lawyer's office in downtown Miami.

All the back-and-forth phone calls and texts message.

They'd all been for this moment right here, and I couldn't let her nerves blow it.

So, I faced her and put my hands on her shoulders and squeezed until she looked at me. "Do you know how much we've accomplished in such a short amount of time? This place is fucking gorgeous, and it's more than I ever thought it could be. After tonight, the residents of Miami and everyone who visits this city are going to be fighting for a reservation." I smiled. "More importantly, the world is going to know that you've landed in South Florida, and you're here to fucking stay." I shook her shoulders and lowered my voice. "I wouldn't be here if I didn't believe in you. You know that."

She nodded. "I know."

"Good. Now, get your ass moving. There are a lot of people out there, waiting to meet the chef of our new restaurant."

A restaurant wasn't something I'd ever intended to invest in. But, after listening to Kristin's pitch and knowing how talented she was in the kitchen, I saw it as an excellent and highly lucrative investment opportunity. It meant I'd be partnering with someone I used to be engaged to, someone who had fucked me up pretty badly, but I just didn't see that as a problem anymore.

I waited for Kristin to smile before I dropped my hands from her shoulders and led her through the rest of the hallway, through the kitchen, and into the dining room.

The Agency's top publicist, the same one who worked with Talia, met us at the door. We had hired her independently for tonight's event, and she had invited everyone.

The media. Local celebrities. The wealthiest residents of Miami-Dade County.

My best friends and their significant others.

They were all here to celebrate the grand opening of Rosemary.

The three of us made our way through the dining room, which had been set up specifically to accommodate the large amount of people who were here. Once we reached the front of the room, we stopped and faced the crowd.

Our publicist handed me a microphone, so everyone would be able to hear me. I tapped the steel casing to make sure it was on.

When I heard the noise echo through our speakers, I waited for the room to quiet before I said, "Thank you all for being here to celebrate the opening of Rosemary. So many people contributed to this restaurant; I can't possibly list them all. Just know that Kristin and I appreciate everything you've done. Tonight, our staff will be passing around appetizers and small versions of our main courses. We encourage you to try everything and to stop by the bar where you can pair the food with our vast wine list or one of our signature cocktails." I looked at Kristin. "I want to thank my partner and our executive chef, Kristin Evans.

Working with you has been a pleasure, and it's been quite an honor to see your dreams come true."

The biggest smile spread across her face, and she mouthed, *Thank you.*

I glanced back at our guests. "Have fun, indulge, and enjoy."

There was a round of applause, and I handed the microphone back to our publicist before I moved toward where my best friends were standing. Brett and Jack both slapped my shoulder as I man-hugged them separately, and I kissed Samantha, Scarlett, and James each on the cheek.

"The place looks incredible," Brett said.

"Top notch all the way," Jack agreed.

"Max," Scarlett said, "I cannot believe you pulled this off so quickly, and you made it look this stunning."

I took the scotch one of the waiters had handed to me and clicked it against each of their glasses. "Thanks, guys. But everything you're looking at was designed by Samantha."

Jack's fiancée was one of the most popular interior designers in Miami. So, when Kristin and I had discussed the details of the dining room and reception area, I'd told her I wanted to hire Samantha to design it.

The end result blew our fucking minds.

"You had a lot of input," Samantha said. "So, I didn't do this alone."

My input had nothing to do with the way this restaurant came together.

That was all her.

"Take the credit," I told her with a smile. "This is your creation, and it's better than I could have ever imagined."

As she grinned back, Jack wrapped his arm around her shoulders and kissed the top of her head.

"I'm so glad you're happy with it, Max. It's become one of my favorite projects."

Brett took an appetizer off one of the waiters' trays and popped it into his mouth. He groaned as he chewed. "What the fuck am I eating? Because it's incredible."

I glanced at the tray before I said, "That's one of Kristin's signature dishes. It's ahi tuna, avocado, cucumber, tempura flakes, ginger, and yogurt."

"James," Brett said as he grabbed two more, "you have to try this."

He handed her one, and she put the entire thing in her mouth.

"Mmm. He's right," she said from behind her hand. "This is unbelievable."

I gripped Brett's shoulder and shook it, knowing there were so many people I needed to talk to tonight, so my time with my friends would be limited. "Let me know if you guys need anything. I'll come check on you in a little bit."

As I started to walk away, I didn't get more than a few steps before I felt someone touch my arm. I turned around and saw that it was James.

"Can we talk?"

I had been expecting this; I just hadn't thought she'd want to do it so early in the night.

"Yeah. Of course." I moved us to the side of the room where it was a little quieter and stood with her against the wall. "How is she?"

She rested her shoulder against the wallpaper and said, "She's healing really well. The company she works for hired a private nurse to help her at home, so she has everything she needs. Her cast just came off, and she has started physical therapy." She shook her head. "It's like she never skipped a beat. She's back to work and everything."

It was a relief to hear that. I had been afraid the combination of her broken ribs and fractured arm were going to keep her off her feet for a while.

I should have known better.

Eve was so fucking strong.

I just wished I could have seen her recovery and this wasn't the way I had found out about it.

"I'm shocked she stayed," I told her. "I thought, once she was approved to fly, she would come home."

"Me, too, honestly. But she's so happy with the doctors who have been treating her, and she saw no reason to return. She'd be doing the same thing here as she's doing there, except she gets to design there."

"But, if she came home, she'd have friends to help her out."

I was no longer on that list, and I fucking hated that.

"She has them there, too, Max. She's become close with several of the people she works with."

I didn't ask her to elaborate.

I'd lost the privilege to know answers like that the moment she broke up with me.

But, fuck, it hurt to think she was there, and I was here.

My stare dropped to the floor, and I sighed. "I tried, James. I wanted to be there."

"I know."

I glanced up and looked at her.

"I wanted to talk to you about something..." Her voice trailed off as Kristin joined us.

She clenched the top of my arm and said, "There you are. I've been looking for you."

"Have you met James Ryne?" I asked Kristin.

"No," they both replied at the same time.

My eyes bounced between both ladies. "James, meet Kristin Evans. Kristin, this is James Ryne."

Kristin stuck her hand out for James to shake and smiled at

her. I could tell she was a little starstruck even though she'd been trying to hide it from the moment she walked over.

"James, it's so nice to meet you."

"You, too," James responded.

But James's entire demeanor had changed. She'd turned cold, and her smile was fucking weak.

Kristin wouldn't notice, but it was so obvious to me.

After they shook hands, Kristin pulled hers away and said, "I'm so sorry to have interrupted you, but Steph is chatting with the reporter from the *Miami Herald*, and she keeps asking for you."

"I'll be right over," I told her.

"It was nice to meet you again," Kristin said before she walked away.

My attention returned to James. "What did you want to talk to me about?"

Her top lip curled just slightly. "You and Kristin are a little cozy, aren't you?"

Her question surprised me.

Although I knew it shouldn't.

I crossed my arms over my chest. "Why don't you ask me what you really want to know?"

The hardness in her expression grew with each passing second. "I want to know if you guys are fucking."

I laughed; I couldn't even hold it in. "Brett didn't tell you, did he?"

"Tell me what?"

THIRTY-TWO
EVE

"JAMES," I said as I answered my cell. I immediately looked at the clock in the kitchen and quickly did the math in my head to figure out that it was one in the morning in Miami. "Are you okay?"

"Girl, I'm fine, just a tiny bit tipsy. Doesn't matter. We need to talk."

I moved the phone away from my lips and said to the nurse who helped me at my apartment in the mornings, "I'm going to take this call in my bedroom," and I started walking toward it.

"I know we promised not to discuss Max, but we need to for a hot second," she said as I got inside my room and shut the door behind me.

Max was a word James hadn't said since I called her from the hospital several hours after I kicked Max out. That was the only time we'd broken the no-talking-about-Max rule I'd made when I moved to Italy.

I took a seat on the bed and pushed my back against two of the fluffy pillows. "Okay. Say what you need to. I'm ready."

"I'd like to think you're not stalking Max on social media, so you have no idea what's going on in his life. But, since I'm positive that you are, I know you've seen him post about the restaurant he's opening with Kristin, his ex."

My chest was pounding, and that wasn't good.

I'd been trying so hard to keep my pulse down whenever I got stressed out. My body still had so much healing to do. Getting all worked up caused setbacks, and that wasn't the path I needed to be on.

So, I gently pushed my uninjured shoulder back to open my lungs, and I tried to slow my breathing.

"I saw," I admitted.

And, when I had, it had been the biggest punch in the face.

First, it was the idea of the two of them rekindling their romance. Then, there was the thought of them becoming business partners.

What the hell did Max know about restaurants anyway?

I was sure he was just doing it to support her, which made my heart race even faster.

"Well, it's not what you think," she said.

I sighed, resting my palm against my forehead, my brain feeling so heavy now that we were discussing him. "I honestly don't know that I care at this point. Whenever I think about the night I caught them together, it makes me sick to my stomach. And then to know he lied about the two times they hung out, and one of those times he was supposed to be meeting me—I just can't, James. It's too much."

"Wait a second." Her voice changed into a tone that told me I was about to get the wrath. "When the hell did you catch them together? And what did you see them doing?"

I still hadn't told James that I'd made a stop in Miami before I flew to Italy.

Since I'd just outted myself, I really had no choice now.

So, I started the story with when I had actually changed my

plane ticket and gone to his house, and I ended with all the tears I'd shed when I checked into my hotel room that night.

"I understand if you're upset with me," I said. "I lied to you about the whole thing, and that makes me no better than him."

"We'll get to that in a second. First, let me get something straight. You heard their conversation and saw the way they were looking at each other, and that led you to believe that things were heating up between them. But you never actually saw them touch or hook up in any way? And, since that night, you've assumed they're together. That's also part of the reason you're upset with him in addition to him being a complete dickhead about not giving you more."

I could definitely tell she'd had a few drinks.

"Yes. That pretty much summarizes everything."

"Eve, if you only had the lady balls to say something to him about Kristin a long time ago, you could have saved yourself some serious heartache."

I looked up from the bed and caught my reflection in the mirror. "Why do you say that?"

"Because I know for sure that Kristin isn't into Max. And Max definitely isn't into her."

I bent my knees and pulled them close to my chest. "How are you so sure?"

"She's married."

I just didn't think that was a strong enough argument, so I said, "And?"

"And, tonight, I met her wife."

"Her...*wife*?"

"Her name is Steph, and she's lovely. She and Kristin met while they were both in LA. They moved to Brazil, and that's where they got engaged. They got married once they returned to the States. Steph is now a realtor in Miami, and she told me their whole story."

Max's ex-fiancée is married to a woman?

"I think I'm missing something," I told her as I tried to connect everything she had said.

"I felt the same way. In fact, I was so pissed when I found out that I chewed Brett a new asshole because he never told me. I mean, he told me Kristin had ended her engagement to Max, and I'd heard she'd cheated on him. But no one ever told me that she'd cheated on him with a woman."

That was a part of the story I hadn't known either.

I thought back to the pictures I had seen on Kristin's social media accounts. They were all focused on her career. None showed any glimpses of her personal life, so there was no way I would have known that she was in a relationship.

"I'm still trying to process this," I told her.

"It took me a minute, too." She giggled. "Just so you know, I came right out and asked Max. I had to. He and Kristin just seemed a little too cozy tonight at the restaurant opening, so I pulled him aside and asked him if he was fucking her."

My eyes widened. "You didn't?"

"Oh, but I did. That's when he told me the whole story. Once I heard it, things just started to make sense. What I thought were lovey-dovey moments between them was really more of a mutual respect for one another. They have a long history, and now, they have a solid friendship, but it's nothing more than that."

I believed her; I just needed to hear it again. "So, they're really not fucking?"

"Hell no."

I moved my fingers to my temple. "I'm definitely relieved to hear that. Admittedly, I was furious at the thought of them getting back together."

"I can tell there's a *but* coming."

"There is because I'm still gutted over all the other issues. He came all the way to Italy, and he didn't even tell me he loved me or that he'd move to LA or that he wanted a family or that he was willing to meet me somewhere in the middle." I took my hand off my head and pushed it against my heart. "I still don't even know why he came."

"He's an ass, and I want to strangle him. And I'll tell you right now, if I'd found out he was fucking Kristin, I would have choked him out at the restaurant."

I laughed as I pictured this happening. Tiny, petite James standing on the toes of her four-inch heels to reach tall, muscular, over-twice-her-size Max.

My bestie certainly had my back.

"At least, now, you can look at his social media accounts and not want to puke at the shots of him and Kristin." She hiccuped. "That's a bonus, I'd say."

She was right.

But those same pictures hurt for an entirely different reason, and that made it just as difficult to look at them.

"You need to go to bed," I told her. "We can pick this back up when you're rested and sober."

"I'll call you after my second cup of coffee."

"Love you," I said and hung up.

I stayed on my bed and held the phone in my hand.

He's not sleeping with Kristin, I repeated in my head.

The two of them were nothing more than friends and business partners.

My heart was beginning to calm down as the relief really started to sink in.

When I glanced down at the screen of my phone, I tried to stop myself from clicking on one of my social media icons and searching for Max's profile.

It was useless.

Within seconds, I was on his page, and I was staring at the picture he'd posted a few minutes ago. It was of Brett, James,

Jack, Samantha, Scarlett, and himself with the caption, *Opening night at Rosemary's.*

Max was in a navy suit with the most masculine silver tie. Both brought out the blue of his eyes. His beard had been trimmed short. His smile was wide and incredibly sexy.

God, I missed that man.

THIRTY-THREE
MAX

EARLIER TODAY, while I had been hanging out in Jack's office, the two of us discussing some of our clients, an alarm had sounded from his phone. He'd turned it off and told me he had to go run an errand and asked if I'd go with him.

I should have questioned what the hell the errand was.

Because had I known it was picking up Lucy, his seven-year-old daughter, from school and taking her to a high-end kids boutique, I wouldn't have gone. I had no fucking business shopping in a store like that, especially in the middle of the goddamn day when I had mountains of contracts to sort through.

But, here I was, in the passenger seat of Jack's car, listening to Lucy go on and on about her day while we drove through downtown Miami. The music that played through the speakers was for her—a pop band with hardly any talent, who had worked us against our old LA agency and eventually signed with them. That made me dislike them even more.

Jack pulled into a spot that was a block down from the place, and just as I got out of the car, Lucy wrapped her tiny hand around mine.

"Come on, Uncle Max. We have so many goodies to buy."

I walked slower, so she could keep up, and after a few steps, she stopped.

"Nope, you have to do it this way." She lifted her front leg and skipped. "That's how we're going to go into the store. No walking allowed. That's the rule. You ready?"

Lucy was the only person in the world I'd skip down Biscayne Boulevard for.

"I'm ready," I told her as I raised my front leg the same way she had, and I took my first skip.

It had been a while. I was a little fucking rusty.

And, to make matters worse, Jack was laughing from behind me.

If Lucy wasn't watching me so closely, I would turn around and flip him off.

"Uncle Max, you need to go higher, like this."

I tried to mimic the way she'd shot up from her back leg and pushed off her toes, knowing I looked like a goddamn fool.

"Higher, higher," she called out, squeezing my hand, giggling at the same time.

The humidity was brutal. Sweat had already started to form under my suit, and the higher I went, the harder it was to hold her hand because of how short she was.

I was never fucking happier when I saw the entrance to the store.

I held the door open for her, and she walked inside, her cheeks red, her smile as big as when I watched one of my musicians go off on a solo jam.

As Jack came in last, one of the saleswomen walked up to us and said, "Is there anything I can help you with?"

"My daddy and Uncle Max are going to help me look for stuff," Lucy said to her. "Thank you."

The saleswoman gave her a warm grin. Then, she glanced at

Jack and me and said, "If Daddy and Uncle Max need some assistance, I'll be right over there." She pointed to the register in the middle of the store.

"We appreciate it," Jack said.

While still holding mine, Lucy grabbed on to her father's hand and moved us, so we stood in front of her. "Here's the plan. I need a new dress for Joey's birthday party and some leggings to wear after dance class and a pair of jean shorts with flowers on them because, the ones I have, I spilled chocolate sauce all over the flowers, and they look like they've been pooped on."

"Did you get all that?" Jack asked me.

"I think we can manage," I said.

I still couldn't believe I was in this fucking store.

Lucy released our hands and pointed to the right. "Uncle Max, you go over there and look." Then, her finger went to the left, and she said, "Daddy, you go there."

She disappeared toward the middle, and I assumed that was the territory she had claimed for herself.

The quicker I found her a dress, the faster I could get back to work.

I could handle this.

As I went up to the first display, I looked directly over it to find Lucy and saw her head bobbing between the racks. "What's your favorite color?"

I needed a starting point. Color seemed the most obvious.

"Titans blue," she said.

I'd seen the way Samantha had decorated Lucy's room, so I should have known better. Lucy's uncle, Samantha's brother, played for the Titans, and Lucy was obsessed with the team. So much so that Jack flew his girls to almost every game.

Titans blue had to be the goal then.

On the first display, the dresses had ruffles and they puffed out like ballerina skirts and they were all in pastels. Before I moved on to the next section, knowing these were all wrong, I quickly peered over at Jack. He was holding a tiny pair of shorts in his hand, and I could tell he was searching for flowers.

The guy actually looked like he was having a good fucking time.

"You really like this dad gig, don't you?" I asked him.

Jack and Samantha had hooked up eight years ago when Jack signed her brother, and they had all been attending the NFL draft. That weekend, Jack had gotten Samantha pregnant, but the two of them had lost contact, and Samantha never told him she'd had a baby. Only this year, Samantha and Lucy had come back into Jack's life. So, even though Lucy was seven, this dad thing was new for him.

He was mastering it like a fucking champ.

He gazed up, and his eyes locked on mine. "She's the best part of my life."

"Really?"

"I'm not shitting you, Max." He glanced over at Lucy, who was doing cartwheels down one of the rows. "She makes my life better, and she's the reason I want to work so hard and hit my numbers and build this empire. Everything is for her."

He wasn't bullshitting me.

I could hear the honesty in every word.

It just surprised me. Jack wasn't the kind of guy who had talked about having kids. Yet I knew he and Samantha weren't going to stop at one.

The same was true for Brett before he had met James. Since they'd gotten engaged, he'd told me more than once about his desire to get her pregnant.

What the fuck is happening to my boys?

I turned, moving toward the next area of clothes. These dresses were in pink and had bumblebees all over them. They weren't what I was after, so I slid to the third rack and finally found the right shade of blue.

I swiped through each dress, looking for one that didn't have so many bows on it, and I came across an outfit that didn't fit in with the others. Something about it was demanding my attention, so I took it off the rack and held it in the air.

"You really don't see yourself having kids?" Jack asked. "Because, I've got to say, the way you are with Lucy tells me you'd be a hell of a dad."

I ignored him, continuing to stare at the tiny navy suit that I was holding in my hand. It was so similar to the one I'd worn to the opening of Rosemary. The tie was silver with thin navy stripes, and it was paired with a light-blue shirt. There were football-shaped cuff links pinned to the top.

It was fucking adorable.

"Man, can you imagine dressing your little boy in that suit?" Jack said as he walked up behind me. "Having him sit on the bathroom counter while you get ready. Having his own pair of fake clippers that he uses on his face, so he can think he's trimming his beard like you. You squirting some gel into his hand, so he can do his hair like yours."

I glanced from the suit, to Jack, and then back.

"You take him to the party he's getting all dressed up for and pull up to the house and watch him get out of the car and run off with his friends. You feel so fucking proud because he's a piece of you, and that piece wants to be just like his dad."

I'd never thought about any of that before.

I'd never held a little boy's suit in my hand and pictured how it would fit into my life.

I'd never even considered the possibilities it presented.

But, as I listened to Jack and as I looked at the outfit, the idea didn't freak me out. It didn't make me want to leave the store, unlike the way I'd felt when I first came in.

What it did was make me picture a scene in my mind.

"How do you do it?" I asked him as I thought of a little boy with eyes identical to mine. "How do you find time to get it all done? Because, shit, I don't know how to balance anything. I had work on one side, and my relationship with Eve on the other, and Eve never won."

"When you're with someone you want to give your time to, it comes natural. You stop strapping yourself so thin. You hire more support staff to delegate to. And you learn how to say no. That's one of the biggest things. I just can't say yes to everything anymore."

That made sense.

But it was never that I hadn't wanted to spend my time with Eve.

I'd enjoyed every second I was with her. And when I wasn't with her, she was on my mind.

It was that I'd made it a choice, and work always came first. In my head, she had been my reward for when I got all my shit done. But it was never done and I never got caught up and I never gave her the attention she needed.

And she sure as hell deserved that attention.

But just because I had fallen short didn't mean she did.

She'd given me so much.

She came to Miami whenever I asked her to, and she did whatever I wanted the whole time she was here. She attended events with me, she constantly watched me work when we were supposed to be hanging out, she listened to business calls because I insisted on answering every one that came in.

She never bitched once.

What had I done for her?

When I asked myself that question, my answer was that Eve had gotten more than any of the women I'd dated since Kristin.

Was that fair to Eve?

Hell no.

I'd given her practically nothing besides sex, vacations, and gifts, and she still stayed with me. I'd gone all the way to Italy and couldn't say the words she wanted to hear. She kicked me out of the hospital and I made no attempt to go back and fight for her.

What the fuck is wrong with me?

I'd ruined everything.

It had taken me this long to realize it.

I sighed, my attention shifting over to the saleswoman, who was approaching us.

"I'm sorry. Someone must have accidentally put that on the wrong rack. It belongs in the boys section on the other side of the store." She held out her hand. "I'm happy to take it from you."

I didn't move.

"Max, you're looking at that thing like you're going to buy it," Jack said. "Hand it to her, so we can find Lucy a dress and go get ourselves a drink."

He was right.

Why the hell am I holding this?

I gave her the outfit, and as she started to walk away, something didn't feel right.

"Hey," I said, calling out to her.

She turned around to look at me.

"I'm going to take it." I reached inside my pocket and removed my wallet and credit card. "Can you get it wrapped up for me?"

She took the card out of my hand. "Absolutely," she said before she headed for the register.

I felt Jack staring at me.

"Do you have something you want to tell me?"

I laughed. "You mean, did I get someone pregnant? Hell fucking no." I glanced back at the salesclerk, watching as she reached inside the sleeve to scan the price tag. "I don't know, man. Something told me I needed to buy it."

"Jesus Christ," he said, sounding shocked. "Ten minutes in a children's store, and I've already got you building a wardrobe for a kid you don't even have."

"Shut it."

"Maybe Eve should start paying me to take you shopping."

I punched his shoulder. "She probably would, too." And then I returned to the rack of dresses, searching for the perfect one in Titans blue.

The tiny blue suit had been hanging in my closet for a week. Every time I walked in to get dressed, I would look at it. And each time, I would wait for my heart to start pounding or for my hands to grab it and toss it into the trash.

Neither of those things happened.

In fact, the more I stared at it, the more I tried to picture a child in my life.

Not like I'd done at the kids store where his eyes had resembled mine.

This was visualizing a balance—thinning out my schedule to be home earlier and leaving a few hours later, spending less time on the road, hiring more staff and delegating.

Even though the idea felt so foreign, it was possible.

And, every time my brain went in that direction, it always came with images of Eve.

I wanted to reach inside my head and pull her out and wrap my fucking arms around her.

Every day that passed that I didn't talk to her hurt like hell.

So, I looked at her pictures on social media. Half of them were selfies, and God, she was gorgeous. She'd show small sections of her face with beautiful scenery behind her. The rest were straight shots of Italy's landscape, and each one came with a heart.

She loved it there.

But I wanted her.

With me.

In the same bed as me every single night.

I want to wake up next to you every morning. I want to eat breakfast with you when we get home from the gym. I want to jump in the shower with you as you're getting ready for work. I want to see your face over candlelight. I want your lips to be the last thing I kiss before I close my eyes.

I wanted the same thing as her.

I was tired of grabbing air and seeing an empty place in my bed.

Something was missing in my life.

It was her.

It was always her.

I knew what I needed to do.

I couldn't do it all today, but I had some time before she returned.

While standing in my closet, my shoulder resting against the little navy suit, I took out my phone and opened a new email.

Eve,
You deserved more.
I know that.
I wish I'd given it to you.
I wish you'd let me give it to you now.
—Max

THIRTY-FOUR
MAX

Unknown: Hi.

Me: Who is this?

Unknown: It's Eve. It's taken me a few days to respond to your email because I just needed a second. It was a lot to take in.

Me: I meant every goddamn word. You've got to believe that.

Eve: I don't know what to say.

Me: I'm the one who needs to say something. But I can't apologize through text. It has to happen in person, so you can see how sorry I am.

Eve: I'll be home in eight weeks.

Me: Does that mean I can't talk to you until then?

Eve: I don't know, Max.

Me: The ball is in your court.

Eve: Hi.

Me: Good morning, Eve.

Eve: I just spilled a cup of coffee all over my shirt. It reminded me of our trip to Napa when I'd woken up so hungover that I did the same thing at breakfast.

Me: That was such a sexy afternoon.

Eve: You must be talking about what happened in the outdoor shower because that hangover certainly wasn't sexy.

Me: I need to build one of those in my next house for that exact reason.

Eve: LOL. The wine here, Max, it's incredible.

Me: I've had it. You're right; it is. Enjoy yourself.

Eve: I shipped a box of clothes back to LA. My return is becoming very real.

Me: I'm not upset over it, baby.

Eve: I didn't think you would be.

Me: But a part of you is, am I right?

Eve: I love it here so much.

Me: Then, you'll just have to go back often to visit. Maybe we can go together.

Eve: James told me she drank me at dinner.

Me: You must be referring to the cocktail I named after you at Rosemary's.

Eve: You know I hate jalapeños.

Me: You're just as spicy as one.

Eve: Okay...but how am I anything like basil?

Me: It's a soft plant. Smooth on the exterior. But, once you bite into it, the flavor plays on your tongue. Yours used to do the same to me. Fuck, you tasted so good.

Eve: The design team is going yachting for a week, so I don't know how much service I'll have. I fly in the night before the wedding. I'll see you at the ceremony.

Me: Good, because I fucking miss you.

THIRTY-FIVE
EVE

I STOOD from the floor where I'd just straightened the bottom of James's wedding gown and tightened the straps on her shoes. Then, I took several steps back, so I could take in the whole picture. "James, my God, that dress is everything." My stare rose to her face, dropped down, and slowly climbed again. "You're seriously one of the most stunning brides I've ever seen."

Over a hundred designers had reached out to me, asking to make her dress. After a week's worth of phone calls, some lasting for hours, James and I'd narrowed it down to three. I'd asked each of them to design a mock-up, which they'd shipped to me in Italy. James had then flown in and tried them on, and we had chosen the one we loved the best.

The winner was an off-white Versace that was made in two layers of French lace. The strapless design slightly cupped her shoulders, ran extremely fitted down the bodice where it cinched her waist, and then bowed just a few inches at her thighs before it ended in a two-foot train.

It was incredibly sexy.

But it was also delicate and soft at the same time.

Lorrie and another makeup artist had been flown to Miami to do James's face and hair. She wore her long strands down in loose curls, and her makeup heavily accented her eyes.

As her maid of honor and stylist, I had the privilege of helping her get dressed. To give her some privacy and a much-needed break from all the women in our suite, I'd taken her into the master bathroom.

She looked at herself in the mirror above the sinks, turning to each side to get a view of every angle. "We did good with this one, didn't we?"

"None of the others could even compare." I walked closer to my best friend, lifting a section of her curls and placing it in front of her shoulder. I checked the backing of her earrings to make sure the diamonds were tight, and I brushed away a stray lash. "Brett is going to die."

"I'm not nervous. Isn't that strange?"

I was.

In fact, I was a wreck.

Since my flight hadn't gotten me in until midnight last night, I'd tiptoed into James's suite, so I wouldn't wake her. Fortunately, she had been up, and we'd had a glass of wine together before we both quickly passed out. But, by getting in so late, I'd missed the rehearsal and the dinner and the opportunity of seeing Max.

I knew he was somewhere in this mansion, and that was goading my anxiety.

It wasn't like we hadn't spoken since he saw me in the hospital.

We'd texted several times, but seeing him was going to be different. It would bring my emotions to a whole different level.

I just wasn't sure I was prepared for that.

"I don't think that's strange at all," I answered. "I think you're ready, and you're confident that this is the man you want to marry; therefore, there isn't a question in your mind. You know you're doing the right thing."

"I love him, Eve. So much."

I wrapped my hands around hers. "I know you do."

"You're shaking."

"I've had too much coffee," I replied, tugging my fingers away.

She laughed. "No, you're a hot mess over seeing Max, but nice try."

"I'm not talking about this on your wedding day."

She stepped closer, wrapping both hands around my arms. "I don't care if it's my wedding day. You're my best friend, and Brett and Max are like brothers. We're going to talk about this, and you're not going to fight me on it."

I rolled my eyes. "I told you last night, we've texted. That's it. There's nothing else to discuss."

"You're about to see the man you're in love with after six months. You're shaking; you're so nervous. You know the two of you are going to end up having a conversation. So, what the hell are you going to say?"

I hadn't thought of that.

I couldn't.

It was too stressful to put my brain there.

So, I said, "I'm not going to say anything."

"Because you want him to do all the talking first?"

I nodded; she was right.

"What if he tells you he loves you?"

I thought of the email he'd sent, which had triggered me to text him a few days later.

You deserved more.

I know that.

I wish I'd given it to you.

I wish you'd let me give it to you now.

He understood the *more* I was after, and he wanted to give it to me. But that email had been sent over eight weeks ago. In man time, that was an eternity. Therefore, it didn't necessarily mean that was what he wanted now, and his feelings certainly could have changed.

"I don't anticipate that happening," I told her.

"Eve, don't underestimate that man."

I scanned her eyes, looking for whatever she was hiding. "Why are you giving Max so many props right now?"

She shrugged, smiling. "Maybe he deserves it."

"Oh God," I sighed. This was her wedding day, so of course she was all about love at the moment. I grabbed her hand and led her to the door. "Are you ready to do this? We have about five minutes before we need to go outside on the patio."

"I'm ready," she said.

I opened the door, and the bridesmaids and glam squad turned completely silent as they all looked toward me. "You're going to die when you see her," I teased them, and then I moved out of the doorway to make room for James.

She slowly revealed herself, and I heard all the gasps.

I took a peek at all of their faces, and they were having the same reaction to her as I had.

While they soaked her in compliments, I went over to Lorrie and had her touch up my makeup and put a few more curls in my hair. By the time she finished, James was ready to leave. Since her parents were no longer alive and her mother wasn't here for this moment, I looped my arm through hers, and I walked her down to the entrance of the patio.

The home James and Brett had chosen to get married at was private, directly on the water, with a grand staircase that wrapped around the back of the house, starting at the second story, where James would begin her descent. The lawn was massive, and that was where the ceremony and reception would take place.

"The groom is already waiting outside," the wedding planner told James. "We can start whenever you're ready."

"Let's do it now," James replied.

We were told to line up in order. Then, each bridesmaid would be paired with a groomsman, and they would walk us down the aisle. I would be going with Brett's best man.

Who just happened to be Max.

Since the men hadn't arrived yet, I took a few minutes to get James settled in the back of the line. I then slipped in the spot in front of her while the rest of the girls went ahead of me.

A door opened, and the men stepped onto the patio. Their shoes ticked on the stone tiles. The scent of whiskey filled the air.

I was too scared to look in their direction.

Too anxious to catch eyes with Max.

Too worried I'd fall apart before we needed to walk in front of all the guests.

But then, the scent of whiskey faded, and a new one wafted up to my nose.

Spice and leather.

It was him.

My heart started to pound inside my chest.

My throat tightened, making it hard to breathe.

My body felt weak as a piece of dark fabric swished across the side of my arm.

He was standing next to me.

His eyes were on me.

I could feel them.

And his heat, too, while I drowned in his scent.

I sucked in as much air as my lungs would hold, and I slowly looked up at him.

Oh God.

His eyes. Lips. That deliciously handsome face.

It was everything I had missed.

"Hi," I whispered.

His eyes briefly dropped down my body, and then they came right back. "Man, you're fucking gorgeous."

He held his arm out for me to loop mine through, and he didn't take a step until I was clinging to him.

But, even as he took me toward the grand staircase, his eyes never left me.

Mine never strayed from him.

And the intensity between us began to buzz.

THIRTY-SIX
MAX

I STOOD ONLY a few feet from Brett as he looked at James and said his vows, but I didn't hear a goddamn thing that came out of his mouth or the words James followed up with. I didn't see them put on their wedding bands. I didn't even know they kissed.

Because, the entire time I was next to him, the only thing I focused on was Eve.

Italy looked so fucking good on her.

Her face was glowing. There was a sparkle in her eyes. Her body was tighter than it had ever been. If she were in pain from her injury, I would never know. That was how perfect she appeared.

I hadn't even felt a quiver of weakness as I walked her down the aisle.

But she had seen my weakness.

It'd happened the second our eyes locked, and hers had seen right through me.

My body always had the strongest reaction to her. This time, it went deeper. I felt that shit right in my fucking heart.

I just needed a chance to tell her.

That moment didn't come for almost two hours.

Following the ceremony, we had to go for pictures. The photographer wanted to get every goddamn shot with every kind of light, using every fucking pose and angle.

But I participated. I turned the way I had been told. I smiled at the camera, and when we were directed to take the women to the entrance of the tent and wait for our announcements, I did that also.

After the band made the introductions, Brett and James hit up the dance floor first while everyone circled around them.

I missed Brett dipping his bride. I missed him spinning her. I missed him going in for a fucking kiss.

Because my eyes never left Eve.

When it was the wedding party's turn to join them, I grabbed two of her fingers that were hanging at her side, and I walked her to the center, right next to her best friend. There, I brought her hand up to my chest, and I placed it on my heart, wrapping my other arm around her.

I waited until her pulse wasn't pounding against my arm, and I felt her take a deep breath before I said, "I've wanted this moment for six months."

A warmth came over her skin. "You mean, even after I kicked you out of the hospital?"

I'd earned that dig.

"Yes, and I deserved you booting my ass out. I had gone all the way to Italy, and I couldn't even give you what you wanted."

"Max—"

"No, Eve, I need to tell you something first." I turned her, trying to make an attempt to at least look like we were dancing. "I fucked up. I knew it then, but I wasn't in the right place to do anything about it. I wanted you more than anything—I never questioned that—but I couldn't give you all of me." I shook my fucking head as I recalled all the mistakes I'd made.

"You have to understand something. When shit ended between Kristin and me, work was the only constant in my life and the only thing I could control. So, I put everything I had into it, and I became obsessed. I wasn't capable of seeing that at the time. Honestly, I couldn't imagine my life any other way."

I held her hand tighter against my chest, my thumb brushing across her fingers. "There wasn't even an opportunity to choose you. Because you, like everything else, came second." My teeth clenched together as I thought about how disappointed I was in myself. "I know that's wrong, Eve. I know that's so fucking wrong, and I'm sorry."

She bent her thumb around one of my fingers and squeezed it. "God, did you fuck up."

"Since I realized it, I've beaten myself up every day about it. I feel fucking sick, thinking of the way I treated you."

"Good."

I smiled. "I don't know how I could go all the way there and not tell you I loved you."

I saw her take in a breath, but she didn't release it.

I knew she was going to sit on that for a few seconds, so I said, "Do you want to know what I've been up to since I got home from Italy?"

She nodded.

"I've been doing a hell of a lot of thinking, testing my mind, putting it in situations to prove to myself how far I've come. Eve, you wouldn't believe some of the shit I've done."

"Try me."

I shook my head, my smile returning. "I bought a suit that would fit a five-year-old."

Her brows furrowed. "You mean, you got the wrong size?"

"No, I bought an actual kids suit and hung it in my closet to see if I could visualize a child in my life."

Now, her eyes were widening. "And?"

"I could picture it. It's something that I want. Not today, but certainly in the future."

Her mouth opened, but she said nothing.

"I'm not done," I told her, watching her pupils dilate, bouncing between mine. "I'm now living in LA."

"What?"

"I have so much to tell you. We're in the middle of finalizing a partnership, and our LA offices are going to merge. I'm going to manage all the agents."

"You moved?" she whispered, her face still so shocked at the news.

"I'm going to get to spend more time with you because I'm not going to be on the road as much. I'm cutting my traveling way back. I want to be in LA with you as much as I can...in our new home."

"Max," she said and paused. "I don't even know what to say."

"I know where I went wrong, and I'm doing everything I can to fix it." My hand rose from her back and climbed to her face, my thumb resting just to the side of her mouth. "I want you to be mine, so I have to show you how much I love you and that I'll do anything to spend every night with you."

Her pulse was hammering against my hand, but I wasn't going to try to calm her down or get her to take a deep breath because I was just as worked up as she was.

"I knew I loved you. I've known that for a long time. I just couldn't admit it to myself, never mind say it to you. But I'm ready to recognize those feelings now. And I want you to know how heavy they are and that they're so fucking strong."

"You're sure you're ready?"

It was an honest question.

And I could tell by her expression that she needed the reassurance.

"Yes," I said. "I'm more than ready to live in LA with you."

"Where are you staying now?"

"In The Agency's condo. I want to buy a house, but I didn't want to do it without you."

She searched my face. "What if I don't take you back?"

"Then, I'd buy one without you. I'm not leaving LA, baby, but I'm also not going to give up on you that easily. If you do take me back, then I want us to buy it together. You need to love it if it's going to be the place where we raise our children."

"Max..." She was shaking her head, her eyes so fucking wide and watery. "I can't believe what I'm hearing."

"I've been waiting months to say this to you. But I knew you needed space while you were in Italy. I also knew I'd have a chance to talk to you at this wedding. And I thought, if you decided to move on, then at least you'd know how much I loved you and that you made me into a changed person and a much better man."

"I don't want to move on." Her voice was soft, but each word was so fucking powerful.

A part of me had worried that I was too late. That I'd blown all my chances at the hospital in Italy. The other part believed she'd come back to me.

"You want me?" Just like her, I needed the reassurance.

She nodded and backed it up with, "Yes."

I dipped my face, my lips hovering right above hers while my hands held both of her cheeks.

"I love you," she whispered. Her eyes closed, and a single tear dripped from them.

I wiped them with my fingers before I said, "I love you more."

THIRTY-SEVEN
EVE

MAX DIDN'T KEEP his hands off me during the entire reception. Mine were just as naughty, grabbing him under the table while we ate, running one across his ass when he walked me to the restroom.

I couldn't get enough.

And it was a miracle that we hadn't fucked by the time the party was over.

But, instead, I was a good maid of honor and he a best man, and we didn't leave until the bride and groom departed for the night.

Seconds after they drove away, Max and I were in the backseat of an SUV, on our way to his house.

As we approached the gate that divided his property from the street, the sight made me smile. It was a view I never thought I'd see again, one that felt so good to drive past.

This time, I wasn't going to surprise him.

Tonight, he was the one who had surprised me.

I hadn't expected to return from Italy and have things go this way.

At best, I'd anticipated it happening in stages. Maybe he'd warm up to one of the ideas, and it would take months or a year before he considered another.

I could have lived with that.

But that just wasn't the case.

I got hope that I would one day be a mother.

I got him moving across the country.

And I got all this because he loved me.

As I sat next to him in the backseat, I leaned against the side of his body while his hands surrounded one of mine. I let my eyes close—not because I was tired, but because I needed to take in this moment. I needed to remember it. I needed my body and my heart to process it simultaneously.

When it came to Max, my body usually got the most attention.

But I'd heard *love* come out of his mouth more than once tonight, and my heart needed to recover from the shock.

Just as I opened my eyes again, I saw that we were pulling up to the front of his house.

He climbed out first and gave me his hand to help me onto the ground. Once my feet hit the brick pavers, he walked me through the front door, past the kitchen and living room, and straight into the master wing. I was only two steps from the entrance when he backed me up against a wall, cupped my face, and brought me as close to him as possible.

"It was torture, having to wait all night to do this," he said.

His mouth hit my neck, and he kissed all the way to my cheek and across my entire chest.

"Max," I moaned.

My nipples hardened, silently begging for his teeth. My pussy craved that perfect cock of his, needing it to be inside my soaked center.

His hands dropped from my face and reached behind me, lowering the zipper of my dress.

It fell to my ankles, and I stepped out of it.

His gaze dipped down my body. "Fuck," he growled.

Four-inch heels, a black strapless bra, and a pair of matching panties.

That was all I had on.

"I'm going to try to be gentle," he said, his stare slowly moving its way back up. "I don't want to hurt your injuries, but it's going to be hard because I want to fucking dominate you."

My nipples achingly pushed against the inside of my bra, and I almost reached down and rubbed my pussy just to give it the friction it was screaming for.

"You don't have to be gentle. I can take it."

"Don't tease me, Eve."

"I'm not."

"Jesus," he hissed, his eyes falling again, this time landing at the dip of my inner thighs. "I need to taste you. Right fucking now." He reached underneath me and lifted me into the air and wrapped my legs around him.

We were moving.

Fast.

And, suddenly, I was on the bed and he was grabbing for my panties and they were yanked off me.

His mouth didn't hesitate. It was immediately on my pussy, giving long licks toward my clit, a finger rotating around my entrance. In a voice that was muffled from being pushed against my lips, he said, "You taste so fucking good." He followed that with dipping two fingers inside me.

"Oh God."

It had been so long since I was touched or had an orgasm from anything other than a vibrator, and the combination of the two was bringing me straight to the edge.

After just a few more flicks of his tongue going back and forth across my clit, I was screaming. My stomach was shuddering, my pussy clenching around his finger.

"That's what I wanted," he growled. "For you to come all over my face."

Once I stilled, he moved out from between my legs, and he knelt in front of me. He gripped my thighs, spreading them so that they surrounded him. Now that I was in the position he wanted, he lifted my ass off the bed, so my pussy was aligned with his cock.

When he inserted just the crown, his head tilted back, and he groaned, "Fuck," so much louder than I'd ever heard him before. "I forgot how fucking tight you are."

I moved my hips, urging him to give me more, my pussy desperate to be filled.

"Tell me how much you want my dick."

I reached down and pressed two fingers against my clit, rubbing them in a circle. I needed the friction, but I also knew how much Max loved watching me touch myself, and that inspired me to massage even faster.

"Don't make me wait," I cried. "I need your cock. Right now."

He thrust all the way in, and my moan blared throughout the room. The same noise poured from my lips when he pulled out and shoved back in.

He was establishing a rhythm, and my body was responding. His hips circled, and his hands dug into my thighs as he continued to hold them open.

"Yes," he grunted. "That's the spot I want."

He had tilted his cock upward, knowing the tip would find that sensitive spot deep within me. At first, he was just tapping it after each pounding of his dick. But then he stayed all the way in, and he ground his hips in a circle, causing him to brush the spot back and forth.

I couldn't hold it in.

My orgasm burst through me, and my entire body began to quiver, the sensation exploding in my clit. "Max!" I yelled.

"I want you to scream out that fucking orgasm," he said, pummeling through each shudder.

So, I screamed, and my body shook as pleasure pulsed through it.

Instead of slowing down, nursing my pussy with his length, he pulled out and pressed it against my ass.

It was a warning.

And then, he released my thighs, flipped me onto my stomach, and positioned me on my hands and knees. "Point your ass out, baby."

I arched my back and spread my legs even further apart, giving him the opening he was after.

Once again, I felt him poke against me, this time his cock running from my ass to my pussy, spreading the wetness and soaking himself in it.

The first thing that entered me was a finger and then a second one. I heard when he added spit, and I felt the thick wetness as it mixed with my own. He pumped me in and out, stretching me, readying me to take him in. And, when he thought I could handle more, his cock went in an inch.

"Yes, Max. Give me more," I demanded, enjoying the small spark of pain I always felt whenever his dick got reacquainted with my ass. It only lasted a few strokes before my body remembered his size and took him all the way in.

He went slow, burying himself fully, and then gently moved back to his crown. I enjoyed the pace. It gave me the pressure I needed. And what intensified it was the way I reached between my legs to rub my clit.

The slowness didn't last long.

Max put his hands on my hips and began to fuck me harder.

That turned into deep, fast, relentless strokes that sent my body to a place it hadn't reached in a long time.

"Baby, your fucking ass feels so good," he roared. "I want to feel you get off, and when that pleasure rips through you, I want you to milk the cum out of me."

The only way I could respond was to moan.

So, I did, so loudly.

And I felt the build work its way into my clit and spread to my ass.

"Fuck," he groaned. "Just like that." He gave me one long, merciless thrust. "Now, take my fucking cum."

My body started to shake, the sensation so intense that each grunt ended in a scream.

"Yes," he said. "Suck it right out of me."

I felt his cock get even harder the second before he shot his first load. Then, each time I bucked against him, another squirt landed in my ass.

When he finally pulled out, he moved me onto my back and cleaned me off before he joined me on the bed. Facing him now, he swiped his thumb across my lower lip. "I have a present to show you in the morning."

"What is it?"

"I can't tell you. It will ruin the surprise."

"I think I've had enough surprises today."

He let out a tiny groan and kissed my forehead. "I hired Samantha to convert one of the guest bedrooms into a closet."

"Why?"

"Because half of my closet isn't enough space for you, so now, you'll have all the room you'll need when we're here on vacation."

I melted from the way he had described this house, and then again as I said, "You built me a closet?"

"No, baby, I built you the most badass fucking closet there is. Even James was jealous when she saw it."

That was why she had been on his side.

She had known everything he was going to do tonight.

My hand went to his face, so I could brush my fingers through his beard, and then I kissed him. "Thank you."

"No need to thank me. You know I love spoiling you."

"But, Max, there's a difference between buying me a bag and building me a closet."

He smirked. "Not really. The kind of bags you like almost cost the same."

I giggled against his lips. "God, I love you."

"Mmm," he moaned. "Say that again, but this time, use my name."

THIRTY-EIGHT
MAX

"MAX, don't you think this is too much house for us?" I heard Eve ask as she stood on the balcony that was directly off the master bedroom.

I finished touring the master bathroom and joined her outside, the French doors opening to a view that I'd been thinking about since I moved back to this fucking city.

A city I was really starting to enjoy because of Eve even though I hadn't wanted to return. I still missed the hell out of my friends, but I was in Miami at least once a month to see them and they were in LA just as often.

"Because it's over six thousand square feet?"

She laughed, shaking her head. "Because there are six bedrooms, a wine cellar, a media room, and a pool, and the square footage is more than double what I told the realtor we were looking for."

Nancy, the realtor I'd hired, had met us at The Agency's condo where Eve and I had been living since we returned from Brett and James's wedding three months ago. Now that Eve's rental house had been converted into an office space for her and Trevor, the condo was the only place where we could stay.

But three months had been enough. I was ready to buy something that would give us more space, that wouldn't have anyone living beneath us, that would allow us to unpack more than our clothes and feel like it was our home.

Eve had given Nancy a list of criteria.

Her goddamn criteria.

No matter how much I spoiled that girl and how much money she'd earned, she was still so fucking humble.

So, while she'd listed off the things she wanted in a house and Nancy had written them down, I'd nodded and smiled and done everything a supportive boyfriend should. But, once she'd left and I'd had a second alone, I'd called Nancy and amended the list.

Whatever Eve had asked for, I doubled. Sometimes, tripled. And I'd told her there was only one location where I wanted to live, and that was the Hollywood Hills, a section of LA that Eve hadn't mentioned.

When Nancy had picked us up from the condo this morning and brought us to the first showing, Eve had been pissed. The house wasn't anything like what she'd asked for, so she'd pulled me aside and accused the realtor of not listening to a goddamn thing she'd requested.

I'd told her I'd handle it, but we were still going to look at the house.

The second place was even bigger than the first.

And, because the realtor had sent me the listings and comps for each one, I was already familiar with the homes. Out of the five we were scheduled to see, I'd chosen a favorite.

We were standing in it right now.

It had everything I was looking for—the size, the upgrades, the wine cellar that I knew she was going to fucking die over.

But I could tell it would take some convincing before she would consider it.

"Truth?"

She searched my eyes. "Spit it out."

"I called Nancy and changed our list of criteria."

"I was hoping that was the case instead of her blatantly ignoring everything I'd asked for because this isn't even in the same ballpark of what I had in mind."

"I know, but I want you to give it a chance."

Her eyes left mine, so she could take in the scenery, the way the homes were built into the Santa Monica Mountains, at how we could see downtown LA from here. "It's hard to hate this view."

I moved her to the edge of the balcony and stood behind her, wrapping my arms around her stomach, resting my chin on her shoulder. "Think of it as your new view."

"Max—"

"I know what you want in a house, but I really want you to consider some of the ones we've looked at today."

It took her several seconds before she said, "Are we looking at any more? For some reason, I feel like you know the answer to that question even though Nancy has said nothing about it."

"Two more."

"And they're better than this one?"

"Not in my opinion."

She gazed to the side, which put her cheek close to my mouth. "I'll admit, this is the nicest of the three."

I tightened my grip around her waist. "And the view is sick."

"There's that, too." She glanced straight again. "I don't see any construction that would need to be done. Just some color changes, getting rid of some of the carpet, and decorating."

I moved my lips closer to her ear and said, "Which Samantha is going to knock out once we close."

"There's just one major problem." She sighed.

"What?"

"It's so far out of the price range we talked about. I knew I could afford half of the house if we stuck with the criteria we gave her, but this"—her finger twirled around in a circle—"isn't even close to my budget."

Whatever house we purchased was where we'd live when we got married, where we'd raise our kids, so I needed her to be comfortable with this decision. At the same time, I also wanted her to feel like an equal in this relationship.

Eve didn't want me to buy the house.

She wanted us to buy it.

My girl did well.

But splitting a five-and-a-half-million-dollar home might be a stretch.

Had she not been so adamant about contributing the same amount, I'd be signing the purchase offer right fucking now, and this conversation wouldn't be taking place.

But, somehow, I needed to make this work, so I said, "I promise you'll be able to afford it."

She turned in my arms, now facing me. "The only way that's going to happen is if you put enough money down that leaves me with a budget I can afford, and you let me mortgage that amount."

I hadn't even thought of that.

I cupped her cheeks and brought my mouth down to hers. "If that's what it takes, consider it done."

I watched her think about my offer. "I don't know."

And then an idea came to me.

As a stylist, she was a visual person. If I wanted her to see this as our home, I had to make her look at it that way.

"I want to show you something," I said, taking her by the hand and leading her back through the bedroom.

When we got out of the master wing, I brought her toward the entrance of the house and up the staircase to the second story. The smallest of the six bedrooms was to the right, and I stopped once we were in the doorway.

"We already saw this room."

I put my hands on her shoulders, and I moved her inside several feet. Standing behind her again, with an arm now wrapped across her chest, I used the other to point to the left wall. "The rocking chair could go right there." I shifted my fingers, aiming at the corner and the back of the room. "Animals hand-painted on the walls. Big ones, like lions and giraffes. Maybe a giant stuffed alligator on the floor." I turned her toward the right. "The crib would go there. In the center. With his name painted right above it." I twisted her one last time, so she faced the closet. "This area is going to need the most work. With all the clothes you're going to buy him, we'll have to blow through the next room to make the closet double the size."

She continued to circle until I got the front of her body.

I noticed immediately that her eyes were a little watery, and there was so much emotion in them.

I pulled her against me, hugging her while I kissed the top of her head.

"What did I do to deserve you?" she whispered.

Since she'd returned from Italy and we'd been living together, we talked about children all the time. Marriage. Where we wanted to live when we retired, how we wanted to build a second restaurant and open Rosemary II in LA. The businesses we wanted to invest in as a couple and how we could financially grow together. I'd come a long goddamn way since we first started dating.

I hadn't just brought her in here to persuade her.

I'd brought her in, so I could see the room one more time and picture where my kid was going to sleep.

When the first tear dripped from her eye, my chest felt like it was going to fucking explode.

I caught it with my thumb, and as I bent down to kiss her, she stopped me and said, "I know where I'm going to put that little suit."

It was currently in storage since we had limited space and Eve had enough clothes for ten closets.

"Yeah?" I said, grazing my lips across her cheek, letting her feel my whiskers. "Where's that?"

She used her head to nod toward the closet. "In there."

I smiled, knowing what that meant.

And, suddenly, a whole different kind of feeling came through me.

"You know, Nancy is all the way downstairs," I growled near her mouth.

"And?"

"And I just want to make sure I like the height of the countertops in the bathrooms."

"Because?"

I pressed my hard cock against her, so she could feel what she did to me. "Because I plan on putting your ass on top of those counters every goddamn day and fucking you until you're shuddering on the stone."

"Max..." Her expression told me she was hesitant. And, by the way she looked between the hallway and me, I was sure she was going to tell me it was a bad idea to fuck right now. Until her lips rose into a grin, and she said, "I seriously don't know what you're waiting for."

God, I fucking loved her.

EPILOGUE

MAX

IT WAS New York Fashion Week, and I was sitting in the front row, inches from the runway, at the Horse Feathers show.

Eve had been in Manhattan all week, preparing for today. I'd only just flown in yesterday, stopping for a few meetings on my way to the East Coast, including one at my realtor's office.

I had picked Scarlett, James, and Samantha up in Miami, and we'd all come in together. Now, they were sitting next to me.

I knew Eve was nervous. This was her first design gig, but I was positive it wouldn't be her last. Word had spread that Horse Feathers' summer collection was something that needed to be seen.

And this place was fucking packed.

Damn it, she was one talented girl.

One hell of a businesswoman, too. She now had three assistants, a real office space, and a client list that was as impressive as my own.

"I'm freaking out for her right now," James whispered, her hand over her mouth so that no one could read her lips.

There were press and paparazzi everywhere. Cameras

pointed at us. Pictures of the four of us were already on every gossip site, and more would be added as we continued to sit here.

"She was so stressed this morning," I replied, my fingers also hiding my lips. "I tried feeding her a shot, and she wouldn't take it."

"That's because her stomach is in a knot." She nodded toward the other side of the runway. "Those are all buyers over there. This show is going to determine what pieces of the collection they want, if any, and how many of those they're going to order."

"No pressure," I said.

She laughed. "Not even a little bit."

The lights flickered, letting us know the show was about to start. Then, slowly, they dimmed until only a glow was left. The runway was made of Plexiglas, and a bright white light shone through it. The sound of dripping water came through the speakers.

The mood had been set.

Now, the first model was hitting the stage. She was in a dark gray dress that had cuts across the top, the fabric sliced and pointed at the tips of her shoulders.

I didn't know much about fashion, especially the pieces that women wore.

My specialty was taking it all off.

But I could hear the reactions around me, the movement of cell phones as they lifted into the air to get a shot, the whispered compliments.

She deserved every one.

What I'd seen so far was incredible. But what I noticed almost immediately was the lack of color among the collection.

White, gray, and black.

That was it.

And why it stood out so much was because Eve's closet in our houses in LA and Miami were like a rainbow explosion.

She had told me the pieces represented the emotions she'd felt while she was away.

I could see our breakup. Her tears.

Fuck, I could even hear her cries.

When the last model left the stage, the first one entered again. She was then followed by the rest of the group, and they circled one final time.

As soon as they finished, the applause got louder, and Eve's moment came. Holding the hand of the brand's owner, she walked onto the stage. She waved at the crowd with the most beautiful smile on her goddamn face.

I stood, my hands clapping together as I tried to keep my emotions under control.

My eyes were fighting hard, trying to fill with water, but I wouldn't let them.

Once Eve and the owner made it halfway down the runway, they turned around and disappeared behind the stage.

James then said in my ear, "Max, our girl fucking killed it."

I nodded and smiled and listened to Scarlett and Samantha have the same reaction, all while the audience continued to clap.

When the lights turned on, everyone made their way to the exit.

The girls and I waited for the crowd to thin before we got up.

A reporter immediately came over to me. "Mr. Graham, Gwyneth Lowry with *E! News*. I'm wondering if we could do a short, on-air interview?" She then looked at James. "Mrs. Young, I'm hoping we could do one with you next?"

I looked at James, reading her reaction, before I acted as her agent and said, "We'd be happy to."

She waved the cameraman over along with a lighting guy, and they got set up. When the cameraman eventually held up his hand, showing a countdown with his fingers, I knew we were going live.

She put the microphone under her mouth and said, "Gwyneth Lowry here, standing inside the warehouse where the Horse Feathers show was held just a few moments ago. With me is Max Graham, music agent to all the stars, and boyfriend to designer and stylist Eve Kennedy, who was a major contributor to tonight's show." She turned toward me. "Max, what did you think of the designs?" She put the microphone near my mouth.

"Well, if you want our introductions to be correct, then Eve is technically my fiancée."

"Well, well, well. A congratulations is definitely in order then," she said. "We at *E! News* didn't know that you two had gotten engaged. Have you set a date?"

I smiled at the camera. "We have a few in mind."

"Any that you're willing to share with our viewers?"

"Not at this time."

"We'll be on the lookout then." She paused, shifting her stance. "Let's get back to the show. What did you think of your fiancée's first co-design?"

"I think the collection speaks for itself. The pieces are unique, timeless, especially with Eve's ability to see both sides of the design process. This show has proven how talented she is in both avenues."

"Will she be designing more collections?"

"You'll have to wait and see."

"Thank you for speaking to us, Max."

"It's my pleasure."

The light stopped shining in my face, and she pulled the microphone away from my lips. "Thank you again," she said off-air.

I nodded, and she moved on to James. While she was getting mic'd up and the girls were waiting for her, I went backstage. Eve was standing with the owner to her right and the lead designer on her left. I'd met them both last night and heard stories about the time Eve spent in Italy.

That only confirmed my stop at the realtor's office was definitely going to pay off.

When she saw me, she turned toward me and rushed into my arms. I picked her up and held her against my body.

"Jesus fucking Christ," I said. "Do you know how brilliant you are? Those clothes, Eve, they were gorgeous."

"You really think so?"

"Yes, baby, and so did the entire crowd. I don't know if you've gotten any feedback yet, but the other designers need to be afraid because you're about to dominate the fashion world."

She pulled her face out of my neck and looked at me, chewing on her bottom lip. "I would die if that happened, Max." She released it and bounced in my arms. "Alberto just heard from one of the top buyers, and they're placing an order that triples the highest one he's ever had."

I set her on the floor, so I could hold her face. "Fuck yeah. That's my girl." I pulled her against me and kissed the top of her head. "After all your hard work, this must feel so good."

"It does."

"You know what's going to feel even better?" I lifted my mouth off her hair and tilted her back, so I could see her face.

"I hope you're about to say a nap and a foot rub because I could use both. I'm beat."

I leaned my lips into her ear. "You'll get both of those when we're on the plane."

"Plane? I thought we were spending another week here, so you could get some business done?"

"We're flying out tomorrow morning."

She pulled away from me and searched my eyes. "Max Graham, what are you up to?"

I shrugged. "I just bought something for us."

"What?"

"A condo."

Her eyes widened. "A what?"

"In Milan."

"You bought us a home in Italy? Are you insane?"

I pressed my lips against her and said, "It's your happy place. Now, it's going to be mine, too."

Have you read ...

Negotiated—*Scarlett's Novella*

Signed—*Brett's book*

Endorsed—*Jack's book*

ACKNOWLEDGMENTS

Jovana Shirley, I love you so hard. Thank you for being so flexible because I couldn't have done this without you. Your support, your knowledge, your love, the way you bring all my words together—there's no one like you and no one I trust more than you. XO

Nina Grinstead, I don't even know where to begin. I said that last time, and I need to say it again. It's impossible to express how grateful I am for you. You're everything—my everything—the most amazing publicist and friend. I can't imagine doing this with anyone but you. Love you so much.

Judy Zweifel, I can't thank you enough for everything you've done or express how much I appreciate you squeezing me in. You're amazing to work with, and I just adore you.

Kaitie Reister, I love you, girl. You're my biggest cheerleader and such a wonderful friend. Thank you for everything. XO.

Letitia, I'm so in love with your work. You nailed this one, lady.

Kimmi Street and Crystal Radaker, my soul sisters. I never would have finished this book if it wasn't for you two. You helped me through one of the hardest periods of my life. You encouraged me to keep fighting. And you gave me the strength to do it. I love you both so much.

Ricky, my sexyreads, I love you.

Extra-special love goes to Donna Cooksley Sanderson, Ratula Roy, Stacey Jacovina, Jesse James, Kayti McGee, Carol Nevarez, Julie Vaden, Elizabeth Kelley, RC Boldt, Jennifer Porpora, Melissa Mann, Pat Mann, Katie Amanatidis, my COPA ladies, and my group of Sarasota girls whom I love more than anything. I'm so grateful for all of you.

Mom and Dad, thanks for your unwavering belief in me and your constant encouragement. It means more than you'll ever know.

Brian, my words could never dent the amount of love you give me. Trust me when I say, I love you more.

My Midnighters, you are such a supportive, loving, motivating group. Thanks for being such an inspiration, for holding my hand when I need it, and for always begging for more words. I love you all.

To all the bloggers who read, review, share, post, tweet, Instagram—Thank you, thank you, thank you will never be enough. You do so much for our writing community, and we're so appreciative.

To my readers—I cherish each and every one of you. I'm so grateful for all the love you show my books, for taking the time to reach out to me, and for your passion and enthusiasm. I love, love, love you.

BONUS SCENE

Do you want to read the moment when Max proposed to Eve? Then, turn the page!

BONUS SCENE OF CONTRACTED

Now that we owned a new house in the Hollywood Hills and none of the furniture Samantha had ordered had been delivered yet, it was the perfect time to take Eve on vacation.

The trip I'd planned was a little over two weeks long.

All of it would be spent in Italy.

At night, we'd be on a yacht that was fully staffed and triple the space that we needed. During the day, we'd explore the culture and scenery in each of the cities we'd cruised to.

I wanted to experience the country the way Eve had, and sleeping on a boat instead of changing hotels every night seemed like the best way to do that.

There were three reasons I had chosen to take her to Italy.

First, she was fucking in love with the place. She'd been talking about it since she returned. And I knew how happy it would make her if we went.

Nothing made me more pleased than seeing her happy.

The second reason was that I needed to know which city she enjoyed the most because I was going to buy us a vacation home there.

The third reason was happening in the next hour now that we'd finished off the day I'd planned.

This would be our second night in Tuscany—a region Eve had said had the most unbelievable wine.

This morning, we'd had a private cooking class. At home, I liked being in the kitchen; I just wasn't able to spend a lot of time in there. But, when my schedule allowed it, Eve and I always cooked together. The chef had taught us how to make homemade gnocchi, which was my request. Focaccia bread was Eve's.

After lunch, we stopped by a winery. We toured the whole facility, and once we sampled their collection of reds, we were led outside. Behind their building was a private area on a hill where a table and chairs and lit candles had been set up, and that was where the owner brought us.

From here, we could see the hills in the distance, the vineyards that covered them, and the olive trees that sprouted randomly in between.

"Let me know if you need anything," the owner said as Eve and I sat in the chairs.

I nodded, silently thanking him, and I reached for the bottle of Sangiovese that was on the table. I poured it into the glasses and handed Eve one.

She took a sip, and then she checked out the charcuterie plate, which was filled with some of the best-looking meats and cheeses I'd ever seen. She was holding the glass of wine against her chest and looking out toward the horizon.

"This is perfect," she sighed.

And it was.

The location.

View.

The beautiful girl sitting to the left of me.

"Now, do you understand why I love it here?"

I'd been to Italy many times before, but none of the visits had been anything like this. Where I'd spent time on a winery and listened to the way the wind moved across the hills. Where I'd rolled my hands through a pile of flour and eggs and potatoes.

Water was usually the view I'd always chosen.

But, fuck, the vineyards were just as pretty.

"I do now," I told her.

It was going to be hard to choose where to purchase a home. Right now, Tuscany was at the top of my list. But, after tonight, we would be headed south to check out the Amalfi Coast, and that was supposed to be paradise.

The smile she had on hit me in the fucking chest. Happiness was pouring off of her, and I'd do anything in the world to keep her feeling just like this.

"God, you're gorgeous."

Her eyes slowly connected with mine, and I took in her whole face.

She wore a floppy hat, her hair hanging across her shoulder in a long braid. She barely had any makeup on, but there was a soft glow on her lips. My stare dropped, and I saw those fucking nipples pushing into the fabric of her sundress. She wasn't wearing a bra, and the dress was low enough that it teased her cleavage.

It was so goddamn sexy.

But so was this look on her.

All natural.

Windblown.

Braless.

"Sometimes, the little things you say hit me the hardest," she whispered.

If that was how she really felt, then I was about to blow her fucking mind.

Even though she turned her head to look straight, I kept my gaze on her.

This was the fucking moment I'd been waiting for.

The one I'd been thinking about every day for the last few months.

In my head, I'd considered the different ways that this could all go down. I'd tried to think of the best way to deliver my question. The words I'd need to say.

How to make it all perfect.

I'd forgotten every bit of it.

There was no way to prepare for something like this.

I had to go with what I was feeling right now.

And that was how much love I had for her.

I stood from the chair and moved over to her, kneeling between her legs. This height put us at eye-level. Her legs tightened around me, and I pushed myself a little closer to her.

"Hi," she said so softly.

She set down her wine. Her free hands cupped my face, and that was when she drew me in for a kiss.

The brisk outside air had cooled her fingertips and the end of her nose as it grazed my cheek.

I could taste the wine on her tongue.

All of it was fucking delicious.

"Hi," I replied when I finally pulled away.

"Thank you."

"For what?"

The smile returned to her lips. "For putting this trip together and bringing me here. For being the most incredible boyfriend. For being someone so easy to love."

"I'm easy, huh?"

She laughed. "Now, you are. I can't say it's always been that way."

I took her hand off my face and held it between my palms, staring at the top of it, at the length of each finger, how they each ended in dark polish.

God, we've gone through a lot.

She was right; it hadn't come fucking easy.

But the journey had all been worth it.

Because it had gotten us here.

And this was the place I wanted to be.

"I love you," I said.

"I know."

Now, it was my turn to laugh, seeing that our smiles fucking matched. "My feelings are so much deeper than the meaning of those three words." I squeezed the center of her hand, my thumb rubbing across the back of it. "Telling you I love you just isn't enough, Eve."

"They're the deepest words I know."

I reached into the inside pocket of my jacket and pulled out the box that had been in there since we exited the yacht this morning. It was soft against my skin. Velvet. Something I never thought I'd hold ever again.

But that had changed.

And, fuck, this felt right.

I set the box on the edge of her knee, holding it between two fingers.

Her eyes fell onto it, immediately filling with tears. "Max..." One rolled past her lid and dripped all the way down her cheek. I didn't have a hand to wipe it with.

"There's one deeper," I said.

I lifted the lid off the box, and as she gazed at the ring inside, her eyes widened, her lips parted, and a burst of air shot through them.

"I know you've wanted more, but that's not enough."

Her stare rose until it landed on mine.

"What I want is forever." I took the diamond ring out of the box, and I held it above her finger. "Will you be with me forever?"

She squeezed my hand that was still holding hers while more tears ran across that magnificent face. "Yes." The second I had the ring fully on her finger, she pulled out of my grip and circled her arms around my neck. She buried her face in the spot below my jaw, her lips pressing against the side of my neck. "I'm going to be your wife."

With my hand on the back of her head, I gently steered her until I could see her eyes. My mouth dipped to hers and stayed there until I said, "I can't fucking wait."

MARNI'S MIDNIGHTERS

Getting to know my readers is one of my favorite parts about being an author. In Marni's Midnighters, my private Facebook group, we chat about steamy books, sexy and taboo toys, and sensual book boyfriends. Team members also qualify for exclusive giveaways and are the first to receive sneak peeks of the projects I'm currently working on. To join Marni's Midnighters, click HERE.

ABOUT THE AUTHOR

Best-selling author Marni Mann knew she was going to be a writer since middle school. While other girls her age were daydreaming about teenage pop stars, Marni was fantasizing about penning her first novel. She crafts sexy, titillating stories that weave together her love of darkness, mystery, passion, and human emotions. A New Englander at heart, she now lives in Sarasota, Florida, with her husband and their two dogs. When she's not nose deep in her laptop, working on her next novel, she's scouring for chocolate, sipping wine, traveling, or devouring fabulous books.

Want to get in touch? Visit Marni at ...

www.marnismann.com
MarniMannBooks@gmail.com

ALSO BY MARNI MANN

THE AGENCY STAND-ALONE SERIES—Erotic Romance

Signed

Endorsed

Contracted

Negotiated

STAND-ALONE NOVELS

The Assistant (Contemporary Romance)

When Ashes Fall (Contemporary Romance)

The Unblocked Collection (Erotic Romance)

Wild Aces (Erotic Romance)

Prisoned (Dark Erotic Thriller)

THE SHADOWS SERIES—Erotic Romance

Seductive Shadows—Book One

Seductive Secrecy—Book Two

THE PRISONED SPIN-OFF DUET—Dark Erotic Thriller

Animal—Book One

Monster—Book Two

THE BAR HARBOR SERIES—New Adult

Pulled Beneath—Book One

Pulled Within—Book Two

THE MEMOIR SERIES—Dark Mainstream Fiction

Memoirs Aren't Fairytales—Book One

Scars from a Memoir—Book Two

NOVELS COWRITTEN WITH GIA RILEY

Lover (Erotic Romance)

Drowning (Contemporary Romance)

SNEAK PEEK OF NEGOTIATED

CHAPTER ONE - SCARLETT

"Scarlett Davis, I wish you'd just give me what I asked for," Hudson said in a sharp voice once I answered my phone.

I hit Speaker and dropped it onto my desk, my hands returning to my computer to finish the email I'd been typing. "You asked for our most up-to-date numbers."

"I did."

I smiled because it gave me so much satisfaction to say, "And that's what I sent you."

Hudson Jones was an attorney hired by Entertainment Management Worldwide, the management company that The Agency—the business I owned with my three best friends—was partnering with. Once the merger was complete, the actors, athletes, and musicians who were signed with us would now have access to managers in addition to the representation and PR services we currently offered.

That was, if the deal ever went through.

My partners—Brett Young, Jack Hunt, and Max Graham—and I weren't budging on the terms of the contract. And to show why we didn't have to, this morning, I'd sent Hudson a breakdown of the revenue we'd earned for the previous two months—the amount of time that had passed since he last saw our books. It included Brett's newest client, an actor earning forty-five million a movie, Jack's recently acquired quarterback who was worth one hundred ten million, and the two pop stars Max had signed to labels, worth fifty million each.

"What you gave me was a forecast. There's no way your revenue jumped ten percent in two months."

Conversations like the one we were having used to only take place between Hudson and our attorney. My attorney would then forward me Hudson's questions, write something irrelevant, and bill us an astronomical amount for the two minutes it had taken him to be the middleman.

I'd put a stop to it.

If Hudson wanted something, he would come directly to me.

And, lately, that had been happening all the time.

"Mr. Jones, I'm not a weatherman. I'm an accountant. The last set of figures you received is real; they're not a projection. But what they do is prove that I have no reason to negotiate any of the terms we're requesting."

"Everything is negotiable."

"We both know that isn't true." I crossed my arms over the edge of the desk and then rubbed at the corners of my eyes. "If you'll excuse me, I have to get back to work."

"Scarlett, there are two items still on the table. The percent of equity my clients want and the buyout terms. We've gone over both, and I highly suggest you take the numbers we've offered. They're more than fair."

This guy.

Since the moment he had first called me, there wasn't a single item Hudson and I hadn't argued about. And, before we'd even spoken, our attorney had tried battling it out with him.

I understood the term *hard-ass.*

I was one.

So were my three partners.

We had high expectations that we wanted to be met.

But this man wasn't just a hard-ass. He was quickly becoming the biggest pain in my ass.

"Let me explain this in words you'll understand, Mr. Jones. What we provided was our final offer. If your clients would like to concede, we're ready to sign. If not, we're prepared to walk. Remember, we didn't approach them. They approached us."

A few seconds passed before he said, "We need to talk in person. I'm scheduling a meeting for Thursday."

I glanced toward my computer, clicking on my calendar.

Thursday was two days from now.

And Hudson practiced in LA, which was on the opposite coast as Miami.

"Early afternoon works best," he added. "I'll have my assistant reach out to coordinate your arrival."

While we chatted, which we'd done only twice, I pictured him to be about forty-five, making him fourteen years older than me. I imagined him bald, even more nasally in person, suffering from short-man syndrome with a horrible case of bad breath.

Once I had his description locked down, I'd envisioned his expression when I told him we weren't caving and again when I won this deal. And, lastly, when I told him his demands were bullshit.

I'd responded to everything he'd asked for up until this point.

Now, I was done.

"That won't be necessary," I said. "I'm not coming all the way—"

"The meeting is in two days, Scarlett. In LA. Have your assistant reach out to mine."

Just as I opened my mouth to reply, the phone went dead.

I pulled it away from my ear and stared at the screen.

That dickhead had hung up on me.

God, he has balls.

I left my phone on the desk and went down the hall, looking inside each of my partners' offices. The only one here was Brett, so I knocked before I opened his door and poked my head in.

He glanced up from his computer, and I said, "Got a second?"

"Yeah. Of course." He waved me in, and I took a seat across from his desk. "You look like you're about to fuck someone up."

"That would be Hudson Jones."

He pushed back from his desk and crossed his foot over his knee. "Fucking Christ. What's his issue now?"

"He's not bending."

He sighed, shaking his head back and forth. "How far apart are we?"

"Five points."

"That's significant."

"Brett, it's what we deserve. Every calculation I've made proves it. Our attorney even agrees."

The heel of his shoe started clinking against the edge of his desk. "We either need to get this wrapped up or squash the deal. But the lawyers are dragging this out, and every day that passes, they make more goddamn money off of us."

I knew how much our attorney would earn off this partnership, and it made me sick to my stomach.

"Hudson wants me to go to LA and meet with him on Thursday."

"For what?"

I shrugged. "I assume he wants us to come to an agreement."

His eyes moved to his computer, and he used his mouse to click on the screen. "I'll be in New York on Thursday."

"I know. Max will be in Vegas, and Jack will be in Atlanta, so none of you are available to go with me."

"What about our attorney?"

I'd thought about this same thing as I walked down the hall toward his office.

"I don't think I'll need him. I won't be there to sign anything; I'll be there to talk."

"No, you'll be there to fucking battle."

I smiled. "Precisely."

"Get what you want, get him to agree, and get this deal done."

I hadn't expected to close out the final round of negotiations. But, since the very beginning, I had taken the lead on this merger. It'd started when the three owners of Entertainment Management Worldwide—Jayson Brady, Blake Dion, and Shane Walker—reached out through email. They'd expressed their interest, and after a bit of research, I'd decided to meet with them. Once I'd had a better understanding of what they were looking for, I'd pitched the idea to my friends.

At first glance, the contract they'd provided looked pretty decent. But, once I'd begun to dig into the numbers and break them down, I had known we needed much more.

That was four months ago.

And it still felt like we were miles apart.

"This is the last chance," Brett warned. "I'm not going another round with them, and neither are you."

By end of day Thursday, I'd know if we were going to gain a partnership that would net us millions, making us the highest-grossing agent and management firm in the country, or if all the hard work I'd put in would be for nothing.

It was all coming down to me.

The only partner who didn't negotiate for a living.

Instead, I was the chief financial officer. I'd been working behind the scenes since the day we opened the business. But I'd grown up with these guys, I'd gone to college with them, I'd lived with them for years, and we'd spent our entire career together.

In that time, I'd learned how to hold my own.

So, if Hudson thought I would just lie on my back and take whatever he gave me in Thursday's meeting, then he'd read me all wrong.

Personally, I liked that position when it involved a headboard and handcuffs.

But, when it came to my job and the livelihood of my partners, I was the dominant one.

Soon, he would see that side of me.

I stood from the chair and moved behind it. "I'll make the right decision for all of us. Don't worry; I won't disappoint."

"You never have."

Don't forget to grab Negotiated, *which is available now!*

Made in the USA
Las Vegas, NV
15 April 2024